FIRES OF JUBILEE

Pfalmer

FIRES
of Jubilee

ALISON HART

ALADDIN PAPERBACKS
New York London Toronto Sydney Singapore

First Aladdin Paperbacks edition November 2003

Text copyright © 2003 by Alison Hart

ALADDIN PAPERBACKS
An imprint of Simon & Schuster
Children's Publishing Division
1230 Avenue of the Americas
New York, NY 10020

Designed by Debra Sfetsios
The text of this book was set in Golden Cockerel.

Printed in the United States of America
2 4 6 8 10 9 7 5 3 1

Library of Congress Control Number 2003105620

ISBN 0-689-85528-1

✳ ✳ ✳

CHAPTER *One*

"Ouch!" Thirteen-year-old Abby Joyner hopped on one foot. Her soles were tough from going barefoot, but the briars growing wild beyond the orchard were tougher. Bending, she pulled up the hem of her homespun dress and inspected her dusky foot. A thorn stuck out from under her big toe.

"Mean ol' pricker," Abby muttered as she plucked it out. Her grandma, Mamie, had sent her to the woods to fetch crocks of preserves from their hiding place. Abby had been so worried about snakes and bears that she'd forgotten about the briars.

A twig snapped, and Abby crouched instinctively. Her heart banged as she stared through the tangle of wild rose and sumac. It was early morning, and a ghost of a mist hung over the meadow. "Who there?" she whispered.

Bears, snakes, soldiers. Abby was scared of them all. Especially the soldiers. Didn't matter if they wore blue or gray. They were all hungry. All bent on stealing food. That's why the crocks were hidden far from the Big House.

Hammond House was a small, isolated plantation nestled at the bottom of the Blue Ridge Mountains of Virginia far from a main road, but sometimes soldiers found their way. Three months ago a ragtag band of Confederates had ridden down the lane on their sway-backed mounts. Their cheeks were hollow, their faces grimy. They'd kicked Mamie and Tissie aside like dogs and snatched the cornbread from the oven. They'd shot the last milk cow and butchered her. Then they'd filled their saddlebags and left, leading Thomas the mule.

Now as Abby hid in the thick growth, she wondered if the gray-coated thieves were back. *What will they steal this time?* The war between the North and South had been raging for four years and there was little left.

Something snorted behind Abby. "Bear!" she screamed and shot into the air. Her feet tangled in her skirt, and she fell in a heap on a dew-sprinkled rose bush, her apron hiked over her head. Heart pattering, she peeked from under the coarse fabric of her dress.

Toby, Thomas's harness mate, stared down at her, his fuzzy ears flapping.

"Toby! You like to scare the apron off me!" Abby scolded the mule. Toby lipped at the weeds stuck in the hem of Abby's baggy dress. She'd forgotten that Pap—afraid the soldiers would come back—had tethered the remaining mule in the tangle.

A thorn in Abby's backside reminded her she'd better get moving. Master and Mistress would be rising, and Mamie wanted preserves for the hoecakes.

"Hold still you ornery critter." Abby grabbed a hold of Toby's spiky mane and hauled herself from the rose bush. Her apron was damp, her hem torn. All because she'd been scared of an old mule.

"Git on." Abby whacked the mule's lean flank. When he ambled off, she was glad to see his belly was round with spring grass. Winter had been too long.

Gathering the skirt of her calf-length dress, Abby hurried through the underbrush, keeping an eye out for the landmarks that would lead her to the hiding place. *There!* She spied two stones stacked on top of each other. To the left of the stones was the willow with the broken branch.

Abby stopped beside the willow and listened for the gurgle of water. Then she followed the sound to the spring. Beyond the willow, the air grew damp and cool, and cedars, locust, and sycamores met the wild brush. Abby climbed over an outcropping of rock. Each time she came here, she walked a different way. Pap had warned her about leaving even a hint of a trail.

Two years ago Pap had found the small spring at the base of a sycamore. Last summer he'd deepened the pool, filled it with rocks so the water ran clear, and hollowed out a shelf in the tree roots. There, each fall of the war, they'd hidden the precious preserves that Mamie and Tissie made from summer's bounty.

When Abby reached the sycamore she lifted her skirt and kneeled beside the glistening pool. Dipping her hand into the cold water, she hunted for the sealed crocks tucked in the roots.

Fetch me some apple butter and peach preserves, Mamie had told Abby that morning. Abby pulled two crocks from the water and dried them on her apron. Before leaving, she counted the remaining crocks. Only five were left. Two months ago Master had hobbled home from the war with one leg missing and a powerful hankering for homemade sweets. Soon the tree roots would be empty.

Holding the crocks tightly against her, Abby hurried from the spring and into the orchard, overgrown with weeds.

"A-bbeee! Chile! Where is you and dose preserves?"

Mamie's bellow rang out over the plantation. Abby raised her eyes to the heavens hoping no soldiers were lurking near. Her grandma's call would bring them running, and there'd be nothing but air to spread on the hoecakes.

Abby trotted past the peach and apple trees, heavy with blossoms, and into the kitchen garden behind the Big House. Her grandpa was in the middle of the strawberry plants chopping weeds. Hunched over his hoe, he reminded Abby of an old gray squirrel.

"Only five crocks left in the spring, Pap," Abby said as she walked between the rows, her bare feet sinking in the spongy earth.

Pap straightened slowly. His face was as dark and rough as tree bark. "That's five more than if we'd left them in the icehouse for the soldiers to steal."

She handed him the crocks.

"Now scurry and change your apron 'fo breakfast. Your grandma and Tissie are cookin' up a mess of hoecakes and eggs." He nodded toward the Big House. "Maybe there 'nough for you, lil' gal. You as skinny as the picket fence."

"Yes suh." Abby stooped to check the strawberries. The clusters of green berries were turning pink. Her mouth watered. Her empty stomach growled. After a winter of dried apples, a fresh berry would be close to heaven.

Hoping to avoid Mamie and her never-ending chores, Abby ran to the front of the Big House. She lifted her skirt and leaped up the brick steps to the porch. "The portico," Mistress called it. Before the war, the portico had greeted carriages filled with fine, hoop-skirted ladies. Now it was home to the swallows making mud nests in the columns, their droppings dotting the planked floor.

In front of the wide entrance door, Abby spun and bowed. Unwrapping her head scarf, she pretended it was a silk handkerchief and waved it at imaginary visitors. "Welcome to Hammond House," she called, imitating Mistress Rebecca. "Coffee and cakes will be served on the veranda."

"What you chatterin' 'bout chile?" Someone swatted Abby. Mamie stood in the doorway, hands on her wide hips. "We ain't had coffee or cakes since the war."

Abby made a face. "I was pretendin'," she said grumpily.

"Well, how 'bout pretendin' you a slave girl who needs to serve Masta and Missus deir breakfast." Mamie frowned at Abby with eyes as brown and hard as acorns. Cornmeal flour dusted one cheek. A gray hair poking from under her head wrap and folds of skin hanging from her neck were the only signs that Mamie was older than sixty years.

"And after breakfas' you help Tissie in de laundry," Mamie added. "Dirty drawers doan wash themselves." Turning, she waddled stiffly back into the house, her breathing labored.

"Yes 'um," Abby muttered. Sighing, she rewrapped her headscarf and followed Mamie into the front entrance hall. The hall was bare except for a rickety table and a lone candlestick used for lighting the way at night. Long ago the rugs had been made into winter wraps, the chandelier traded for molasses and salt.

Abby glanced up the winding staircase, catching her breath when she saw Mistress Rebecca. Head high, her hand lightly touching the railing, Mistress floated down the steps as if she was wearing yards of satin instead of threadbare calico.

Before the war, Violet, Mistress's personal servant, had brushed and pinned Mistress's hair, fastened and laced her corset and petticoats, and powdered and rouged her face. But two summers ago Violet had run off. Now, except for the chamber pot left outside the door each morning, Mistress cared for herself.

Abby curtsied. "Mornin' Mistress."

"Good morning, Abby," Mistress said. "Were you rounding up the hogs this morning?"

"Ma'am?" Abby looked up, confused.

Mistress pointed to the stains on Abby's apron and

the rip in her hem. "By the look of you, I thought perhaps you'd been fetching hogs."

Abby felt the heat rise in her cheeks. "No Ma'am. I was fetchin' preserves for Master's breakfast."

"That's nice. Now see that you change before serving. Master will be down shortly." Mistress's gaze shifted to the spiral staircase, and worry lines creased her brow. Every day Master struggled with the long, winding stairs. Once Abby had suggested to Mamie that Master use the shorter slave stairway, but she was only rewarded with a slap.

Mamie's answer to everything, Abby thought as she hurried down the hall and up the narrow wooden stairs. That was one reason Abby had stopped asking questions about her own Mama, who had disappeared when she was a babe. She was tired of Mamie cuffing her.

Pausing at the top of the stairs, Abby listened for the thump of Master's crutch on the wooden floor as he paced in his bedroom. Ever since he'd come home to Hammond Plantation, Master had been a ghost of a man.

"Like he lost his soul in the war," Pap had explained. "Then lost his heart when he heard that Miss Julia had died."

Miss Julia. Abby missed her too. Since the little girl had died last winter from scarlet fever, laughter had been as scarce as sugar.

Abby checked to make sure Master wasn't coming, then darted into Miss Julia's room. It had changed little since her death. Abby's straw-filled pallet was still on the floor by the canopy bed since Mistress had continued to let her sleep upstairs.

'Cause Mistress afraid to be alone with the haunts, Pap had explained. And now that Master was home, Mistress was grateful for help at night when her husband began rambling feverishly.

Lifting the lid of the small wooden trunk at the head of her pallet, Abby found a clean apron. As she tied it on, her attention strayed to Miss Julia's books. Miss Julia's favorite had been *The History of Little Goody Two-Shoes.* Often they'd read it together late at night under the comforter. Abby glanced toward the doorway to make sure no one was in the hall then pulled out a geography book.

Geography, the study of the earth and its people, she heard Teacher's voice in her head. Quickly, she leafed through the pages and found the card engraving of New York City that Teacher had tucked inside. Fascinated as always, she stared at the tall buildings. Abby had never set foot off the farm, but one day she aimed to leave for a big city like New York and find her Mama.

"Hey, Abby, whatcha doin'?" Abby jumped a foot in the air. Cyril, Tissie's seven-year-old son, was standing in the doorway staring at her with big eyes. "I'm readin,'" Abby whispered. "So hush 'fore Master hears you."

"Kin I read, too?" Cyril asked as he scuttled over. Abby wrinkled her nose. One of Cyril's jobs in the Big House was emptying the chamber pots.

"You doan know how to read," Abby said. "Teacher only taught me and Miss Julia. But you can look at this picture." She showed him the photo. "That's where the Yankees live. Crowded together like chickens in a coop. Lookee, there ain no trees or grass." She shook her head. "I doan know what their cows eat."

Cyril shook his head too. "That city place is might poor. No wonder dem Yanks want to live in Virginy."

"That's what Miss Julia used to say: 'Those bluecoats tryin' to steal our home!'" Abby imitated her little mistress.

"Well, if dem Yanks come here, I's tell dem they cain't have Virginy." Cyril puffed out his skinny chest. "I's tell dem dey cain't have *me*. *I* wants to stay in Virginy. I doan wants to be free."

Slamming the book shut, Abby made a sound of disgust. "Not be free!" She slid the book back on the shelf. "That's the foolest thing I've heard you say, Cyril. If you're free you can go to school. You can travel to town without a pass. And . . ."—she gave him a sly look— ". . . you can tell Mistress to empty her own chamber pot."

Cyril's brows shot up. "Den I wants to be free!"

"Don't say 'den,' Cyril," Abby corrected. "It's 'then.' When you free you gotta talk like a free man."

Thumping in the hall told Abby that Master was headed downstairs. "I gots to go," she whispered. "And you skeedaddle, too, 'fore your ma finds you dawdlin'."

Cyril ran out the door. Abby took one last look at the books before hurrying after him. She didn't tell Cyril what being free *really* meant. It meant that Abby could leave Hammond Plantation and look for her Mama. It meant she could find the answers to the questions burning in her heart: Where was her Mama? Why did she leave? *And why will no one ever talk about her?*

CHAPTER *Two*

* * *

"Where you bin chile?" Mamie demanded when Abby hurried into the summer kitchen. The small room, warm and sooty from the brick fireplace, was bursting with the smell of fried eggs and corn meal.

Her grandma thrust a serving tray into her hands. "Git along. Masta and Missus waitin'."

"Yes 'um." Abby took the tray, stuffed a hoecake in her mouth, and hurried down the brick walkway to the Big House. Before entering the dining room, she peeked through the half-open doorway. Master and Mistress sat at opposite ends of the long mahogany dining table. Only two chairs and a sideboard were left in the once ornate room. In early spring, Mistress and Jake the coachman had taken a wagon full of furniture to

Tomasford. Mistress had returned alone driving a near empty wagon. The furniture had been traded for seed, and Jake had run off.

Mistress's back was toward Abby, but she could hear her talking. At the other end of the table, Master sat slouched in his chair, his eyes on his empty plate.

Masta Hammond the comeliest man in all Nelson County, Mamie used to boast proudly. Now his dirty hair straggled across his forehead and his face was weary with grief. *As if the war drummed the handsome right out of him,* Abby thought.

Suddenly, Mistress's voice rose angrily. Abby stopped chewing her hoecake and listened. Usually breakfasts were silently endured. Master shoveled food into his mouth as if he was a starving soldier while Mistress politely and carefully cut each meager bite. But today Mistress was going on and on. Abby pricked her ears, trying to catch the words, but they fired down the table like bullets.

Abby gulped the last of the hoecake. Quiet as a possum, she padded across the plank floor. When she reached Mistress's side, she held out the platter. Instantly, Mistress quit talking and slid something into her lap. Abby heard a crinkle and glimpsed folded white papers. *Is Mistress hiding something?* she wondered.

"Abby, don't stand there like a stump." Mistress

sounded ruffled. "Serve me, please, before the food gets cold."

"Yes Ma'am." As Abby spooned eggs onto the plate, she stole a glance at Mistress's lap. A corner of white peeked from the folds of her skirt. *Is she hiding a letter?* Yesterday, Preacher Thornton had visited Hammond House, riding up on his sickle-hocked bay. Spring and summer, the preacher from Massies Mill rode from farm to farm, carrying news of births, deaths, Jesus, and sinners. Since callers were sparse, his arrival was anticipated by all.

But Preacher's visits usually didn't bring secrets. Master, Preacher, and Mistress usually talked in front of Abby and the other slaves like they had no ears.

So what is Mistress hiding today?

As Abby slid a hoecake onto Mistress's plate she thought back to Preacher's visit yesterday. He'd only stopped for a short while. Since Abby had been throwing corn to the hogs, Tissie had served dinner, and Preacher had left directly after. If there'd been any exciting news, it would have spread like flies from the Big House through the slave quarters. *What did I miss?* Abby wondered.

"Abby!" Mistress's sharp tone made her jump. "Step lively, please. Serve Master Hammond, then you're dismissed. I'm sure Mamie has chores for you. Today's wash day."

"Yes, Ma'am." Abby scurried around the table, her ears ringing. *You're dismissed!* Every day Abby waited silently through the meal, scuttling to attention if Master or Mistress beckoned for more jam or hot tea. When they finished eating, she cleared the dishes.

Abby cou' ln't remember *ever* being dismissed. *What is going on?*

"Hoecakes, Master Hammond?" Abby stopped by his chair, careful not to bump the bandaged stump poking from the seat.

Without looking up, Master nodded. Abby served him, then hurried outside and into the kitchen. Mamie and Tissie were huddled by the fireplace, their heads together.

"Mistress has a secret!" Abby announced excitedly. Instantly, the two women sprang apart. Tissie began scrubbing the plank tabletop. Mamie bent to stir the cook pot hanging over the flames. Neither expressed interest in Abby's announcement.

"Mamie, *what* is goin' on?" she demanded.

"Forgive me, Lord," Mamie murmured to the ceiling before saying, "Chile dere ain nothin' goin' on."

Abby frowned as she set the tray on the table. *Mamie is lying.* Her grandma always asked the Lord's forgiveness before telling a lie.

Must be everyone's keeping secrets, Abby huffed to herself.

Master. Mistress. Might be secrets swarming through the house like pesky ants!

A movement under the table caught her eye. Abby spied a scruffy pant leg and bony ankle. *Cyril. Has he been listening in on Mamie and Tissie?*

Scooting closer, Abby poked him with her bare foot. "Hey, boy. You spyin'?"

With a yelp, Cyril scrambled from under the table and fled out the back door. Abby took off after him, tackling him in the pile of bedclothes Tissie had waiting in front of the wash shed.

"I ain gonna tell! I ain gonna tell!" Cyril squealed like a poked hog.

"Tell what?" Abby demanded as she wrapped him in a cocoon of Mistress's sheets.

"Tell dat Joseph and Able done gone!"

"Gone! When?" Abby lay hard on top of him till he quit struggling.

"Gone las night," he said, panting under her weight. "This mornin', when Uncle Zee woke the field hands, Joseph's and Able's beds were cold."

So that's what Mamie and Tissie were whispering about! As soon as the weather had warmed, the slaves had started stealing away. Now Uncle Zee, the field boss, was down to ten hands. Joseph and Able were two strapping bucks. Without them the crops would be poorly tended.

"What else you hear from Mamie and Tissie?" Abby asked, knowing there was something more. Something hidden in Mistress's lap.

Cyril's eyes grew round as moons. "Uncle Zee was fired-up mad. He say, 'Send the patrollers after Joseph and Able.'"

Abby felt Cyril shiver beneath her. Thoughts of the patrollers struck fear in every slave. Poorly clad farmers and wounded ex-soldiers, the band of white men roamed the hills looking for any excuse to cause a black man trouble. Gabe, Abby's own Pa, had been killed by the patrollers thirteen years ago before she was born.

"What did Mistress say?" Abby asked.

"She say, 'Git the patrollers, Zee. We need those hands for plantin' and tillin'. Only . . .'" Cyril dropped his voice low. "Only Master tell Uncle Zee *no* patrollers."

Abby's ears pricked. *So that's why Mistress was so mad at breakfast!* For three years, while Master was off fighting the war, Mistress had held the farm together. She knew the crops were life. She knew that without them, no one would survive the coming winter. But now that Master was home his word was law, even though his mind drifted for days like passing clouds.

Freeing his trapped arm, Cyril pinched Abby's shoulder. "Now let me go or I tells my ma!"

"Go tattle to your ma," Abby said as she jumped to

her feet. "And I'll tell Tissie your big ears been sneakin' round the kitchen!"

Cyril wormed from the sheets just as Tissie came from the kitchen carrying a basket. With a squawk of fear, he leaped over the picket fence and took off into the garden.

"Cyril!" Tissie hollered after him. "Git back here lazy boy. We gots clothes to wash!"

Abby laughed. "He ain comin' back. He hates washin' more than a beatin'."

Tissie cast her a dark look. "Hush your laughin'. I know you been fillin' his head with words 'bout freedom."

"What's wrong with that? Able and Joseph set on being free. Why not Cyril?"

Why not me?

Tissie plopped the basket on the ground. "You hush your mouth 'bout freedom. Able and Joe young bucks, and even they end up strung in a tree by the patrollers. That's why your grandma didn't want you to know dey run off. She say your fool head already filled with 'nough silly notions. 'Sides, Cyril too young to hear 'bout freedom. He thinks it means he doan have to mind his ma."

"That's still no reason to keep secrets," Abby said sullenly. Reaching into the basket, she yanked out

Mistress's chemises and drawers. Last night she'd helped Cyril, Pap, and Tissie fill the washtubs, hauling bucket after bucket from the well till her arms ached. In the early morning, Pap had kindled the coals beneath the tubs and now the water was steaming.

Abby sighed as she threw the underclothes into the first tub. Washing meant a whole day of boiling, stirring, wringing, and hanging. Tomorrow would bring ironing. The thought made freedom seem far away.

"'Sides," Tissie continued, her voice sharp. "You ever ask what freedom is? You ever ask what Joe and Able runnin' *to*?" She made a noise of disgust in her throat. "They runnin' like fools toward freedom like it was some town. You ask me, freedom ain nothin' but an ugly word the Yankees made up to steal the slaves from the farms."

Abby stared at Tissie. *Freedom an ugly word? How can Tissie think that?*

"Does freedom mean you turn into a white lady so someone serve you and feed you?" Tissie ranted on. She was sorting clothes, bitterness puckering her mouth. "Does freedom mean a new house and fine jewels? No, freedom jest mean you a colored girl starvin' alone."

"Tissie, you doan really believe that do you?" Abby gasped.

"Like I believe in the Lord," Tissie stated firmly.

Abby blinked. "But if you were free you could find Rufus!"

Tissie snorted. "You know nothin' of husbands, Abby. Nothin' of hurt. You jest a chile. Since I bin here, Masta and Missus treat me fair. And dey promise to keep Cyril with me. So quit moonin' over a word and gits to work."

As Abby picked up the smooth stirring stick, she stole a glance at Tissie, who'd come from a plantation near Charlottesville six years ago, baby Cyril in her arms. Rufus, Tissie's husband, had been a slave on the same plantation. His owner had branded him a 'trouble-maker' and sold him south to the rice plantations. Abby had seen the scars on Tissie's back from her old Master's beatings. He'd sold her too when she'd tried to take off after her husband. Now Tissie was alone with her child, tied to Hammond Plantation like the other slaves who were too young or too old to run.

But that didn't mean the strong like Joseph and Able shouldn't run. No matter what Tissie said, Abby felt that in her heart. Freedom wasn't an ugly word. It was as beautiful as reading a book, eating honey on fresh bread, and finding her Mama.

She closed her eyes. As she stirred, steam rose from the hot water and beads of sweat rolled down her temples.

Lord, give Able and Joe the strength to make it north. Let them find freedom, where ever it be. And one day let me find my—

"Girl, look alive now." Tissie broke into Abby's prayer. "Run and git Masta's bandages. There's a pile stinkin' in the upstairs hall."

Letting go of the stick, Abby raced around the summer kitchen and into the Big House. Pausing in the doorway, she peeked into the dining room.

Master and Mistress were gone. And they'd taken their secret with them.

Able and Joe might have run off. And Master may have said 'no patrollers.' But that's not what Mistress had been hiding in her lap. Abby was sure of it.

Abby's bare feet made no sound as she tiptoed into the entry hall. Across the way, Master and Mistress were in the parlor. Abby sneaked a look from behind the doorjamb. Mistress was writing at a desk. Master sat on a ladder back chair staring with vacant eyes out the window.

Silence filled the room.

Abby's gaze lighted on the desk. By Mistress's elbow was a folded newspaper.

Abby caught her breath. Could *that* be what Mistress had slid into her lap during breakfast? Had Preacher Thornton brought her a paper from town? What news did it bring that couldn't be shared?

Mistress knew Abby could read. She'd never told Teacher to include Abby in Miss Julia's lessons—it was against the law for a slave child to be taught—but she'd actively made it possible.

"Abby, fan Miss Julia during lessons."

"Abby, help Teacher clean the slates."

"Abby, keep the flies from the tablet."

And Abby had learned.

If Mistress was hiding the newspaper it was because she was afraid Abby would read it and find out the secret.

And Abby would. She just had to find a way.

***

CHAPTER *Three*

"Cyril, you stand right here." Putting her hands on Cyril's skinny shoulders, Abby set the boy in front of the parlor doorway.

It was evening. The house was shadowed and quiet. All day Mistress had ranted about Able and Joseph. Uncle Zee had gone after them with the hounds but lost their scent at the river. Now Master and Mistress were walking down to the slave quarters to make sure the remaining field hands were in their cabins for the night. Abby knew this might be her only chance to read the newspaper.

"Now doan move," Abby warned Cyril. "Keep your eyes out for Mistress. If she comes, you whistle."

Cyril puckered his lips. "Like dis?" A whooshing squeak came out.

"Jest like that. Whistle then run hide so she doan see you."

Cyril nodded. Abby knew he was too squirrelly to stand long so she scooted into the parlor, carrying a dust rag. She suspected the newspaper was on the desk hidden under letters and receipts.

Receipts.

That word had taken a whole day to cipher out. Abby had listened carefully while Mistress complained to Master about the worthless *receipt* from the Tuckers who lived on the neighboring farm. Since Abby knew how to read the word *receive,* she could figure out *receipts.* Then she'd found Mistress's receipts on the desk when she was supposed to be dusting. That's how she knew why Mistress's heart-shaped jewel box was almost empty.

One ruby ring in receipt for two tins of leavening.

One pearl necklace in receipt for one sack corn flour.

Mistress's jewels had kept them from starving last winter.

As Abby rifled through the papers on the desk, she glanced at Cyril who was hopping from one foot to another like a chicken with chilly feet. Finally her fingers touched the thicker sheaf of pages that told of a folded up newspaper. Mistress had tucked it under the Bible.

Abby hesitated before sliding it from under the heavy, leather bound book. *The Lord will understand.*

She unfolded the newspaper. The biggest words told of BURNING, DROUGHT, and FREEDOM. The sight of FREEDOM brought tears to Abby's eyes. Since the first time she'd seen the word in Miss Julia's reader, she'd held it precious in her head. After, she had etched it into the dirt with a stick and written it in the dust with her finger. But her letters had been as crooked as twigs and these were as fine as lace.

"Freedom Brings Woes" Abby read, her lips moving as she sounded each word. Her forehead bunched. *Who was free? And why did it bring them woes?*

Holding the page by the window to catch the fading light, Abby stumbled over the words. Slowly, haltingly, she read, and as she read, her mind realized what the article was saying.

The war was over.

The north had won.

The slaves were free.

And they'd been free long enough to have woes.

Abby's fingers tightened on the paper. The slaves were free and Mistress hadn't told them! For how long? She searched the page. A date leaped out at her: April 9, 1865. The South had surrendered.

Over a month ago! She lowered the paper, thinking

back to the middle of April. Master and Mistress had gone into town. Did they know then about the war ending? Had they brought freedom with them from Tomasford? If so, why hadn't she seen it?

Because she'd been in the fields.

By April, there were few hands left and only one mule, so Mistress had ordered the house slaves into the fields. For weeks everyone except Mamie and Pap had been stooped over a hoe, sun up to sun down, turning the soil and planting. By nightfall, Abby had been so sore and tuckered out she'd fallen dead tired onto her pallet. No wonder she hadn't noticed Mistress's secret.

Freet-freet. A strangled whistle came from the hall followed by silence. Abby folded the newspaper in half and slid it down the bodice of her dress. *I'm jest borrowin' it,* she told herself. She could hear Mistress's voice on the front porch. Any second the door would open, and she would come inside.

Dropping to her knees, she whooshed the dust rag under the settee, the newspaper poking into her ribs with each stroke. The front door opened. Lantern light illuminated the hall and filled the parlor.

"Abby! You startled me," Mistress said from the entryway. "What are you doing on the floor?"

"Mice," Abby said. "I chased them from the kitchen. They bin rustlin' in the cornmeal sacks."

Mistress sighed. "Oh, will the problems ever cease." Abby heard the thump-thump of Master's crutch as he headed up the stairs. She crooked her head so she could see Mistress, who was lighting the candle in the hall. A light shawl drooped from her shoulders and lines furrowed her brow.

Only once had Mistress ever hit Abby. When Miss Julia was burning with fever,. Abby hadn't obeyed quickly enough with a cool rag, and Mistress, sharp with her daughter's pain, had slapped her. When Julia had died, everyone in the household had shared Mistress's sorrow, and Abby had forgiven her for the slap

But now anger hardened Abby's heart. Master and Mistress had been living a lie for too many days. Able and Joseph needn't have stolen from the farm like thieves. They could have stridden proudly down the lane.

Abby was bursting to run and tell Mamie and Pap. *The war's over! We're free!* The news would spread like lightning through the slave quarters. Young and old would pack up and flee like the flocks of robins that headed north each spring. The crops would wither and die in the fields. The fires would grow cold in the Big House, and Mistress would be furious. She'd know it was Abby who'd told. But no slap could keep the secret inside her.

Abby watched Mistress pick up the tin candleholder and start up the stairs. "See that the doors are latched and the fire banked, then go to bed, Abby," Mistress said, her voice as heavy as her tread on the steps.

"Yes Ma'am."

When the stairway grew dark Abby jumped to her feet. Holding the newspaper against her chest, she ran from the Big House and into the summer kitchen. For once, Pap's tales of haunts didn't make her jump at every shadow. She was too filled with *freedom*.

Abby had little to pack. By morning, she'd be on the road, walking northeast to Charlottesville, a big city she'd heard of but never seen. There she'd begin the search for her Mama.

Bursting with joy, Abby hurried through the kitchen, her path lighted only by the coals of the fire. A brighter glow came from the doorway of Mamie and Pap's room, which opened into the kitchen. Once a supply room, Mistress had had it fixed up for Mamie when she grew too stiff to climb the two flights of stairs to the attic loft.

"Mamie! Pap! We's free!" Abby exclaimed as she burst into their room. Pap was sitting on the edge of the bed darning a sock. Mamie was in her rocker, stitching a torn hem. A rag rug covered the plank floor, a thick quilt lay on the bed. A stubby tallow candle on an upended crate lighted the space between them.

Without looking up, Mamie humphed. "We's free when all the mendin's done. Dat might be 'bout midnight."

"No. We's really *free*," Abby insisted. Grabbing Mamie's right hand, she stilled the needle. "We's no longer slaves!"

Pap dropped the sock in his lap. Mamie frowned up at Abby, the candle flame flickering in her tired eyes. "What you chatterin' 'bout, chile?"

Quickly, Abby pulled the newspaper from her bodice. "Lookee here." Opening the fold, she pointed to FREEDOM BRING WOES. "Mistress bin lying. The war bin over for 'most thirty days. The Yankees won! And to think this mornin' I was hidin' from soldiers. Only there ain no soldiers!"

Mamie frowned at the paper then looked up at Abby, her eyes unblinking. Pap sat as still and hushed as a scarecrow.

"Abby, you know Pap and me cain't read," Mamie finally said. "If you be tauntin' us, chile—"

"No, Mamie! It say it right here!" Abby shook the paper under her nose. "That's the secret Mistress been hidin'. She and Master knowed since April when they went to town!"

Waving the newspaper over her head, Abby twirled

in the light of the candle. "We's free! We's free! We's *free!*" she sang.

"Hush!" Mamie grabbed Abby's wrist and yanked her to a stop. "You hush!"

Startled, Abby froze. She'd expected Mamie to be as excited as she was. Instead, her grandma leaned forward and whispered, "Bank the fire for the night and doan talk of this to a soul. Pap and me pray on this. The Lord will tell us what to do."

Abby wrenched her arm from Mamie's grasp. "The Lord woan tell *me* what to do! Now that I's free, I have no master!"

Mamie slapped Abby so hard her head snapped sideways. Her hand went to her cheek and tears filled her eyes.

"I woan hear such blasphemy." Mamie's voice trembled. "Now mind what I say—leave this to the Lord and pray he didn't hear you."

Dashing from the room, Abby stumbled over a pile of kindling. *Forget bankin' the dang fire. The almighty Lord can light it in the morning.*

Abby raced down the brick walk and into the Big House. The rooms and stairway were dark, but she knew every corner and creak. When she reached Miss Julia's room, she fell onto her pallet and curled into a tight ball. Her heart drummed against her ribs, and her cheek stung.

Tears of anger and frustration spilled onto her quilt. Mamie had said to leave freedom in the hands of the Lord. But it seemed to Abby that the Lord had been deaf to the slaves' prayers for too long.

She could hear Preacher's booming voice as he read from the Bible at the last service, "Slaves, submit yourselves to your masters with all respect, not only to those who are good and considerate, but also to those who are harsh."

Abby had listened in disbelieving silence. Later, Pap told her that Preacher was reading from the white master's Bible. But Abby had found the same words in Mamie's Bible. Besides, the Lord had taken her Pa and Miss Julia, who were both buried in the family cemetery. And he'd stolen her Mama from her as well. *That* Lord would never heed a slave girl's prayers. She'd have to find freedom herself.

Tears streamed down Abby's cheeks. Balling the edge of her quilt in her fist, she wiped her face dry. In thirteen years, she'd never set foot off Hammond Plantation. All she knew of the world came from tales around the fire in the quarters.

But somehow she had to find the spine to leave and look for her Mama.

Tiredness stole through Abby, and her eyes grew heavy. She was almost asleep when a breeze wafted

through the window over her head, bringing the chir-
rup of the spring peepers and . . . *something else.* Opening
her eyes, Abby hushed her breathing and listened.

Singing! She scrambled to her knees. Elbows on the
sill, she stared into the night. The singing was coming
from the slave quarters.

Abby cupped her hands behind her ears. The voices
grew louder and she could make out the faint words:

"Slavery gone away
The war be won
Freedom's here to stay
Jubilee's begun."

The others knew! The Lord must have heard Mamie
and Pap's prayers! He must have told them to spread the
news of freedom! Now *everyone* would know it was a
beautiful word.

Sitting back on her heels, Abby rested her chin and
arms on the sill and listened to the sweet song of
Jubilee. Her eyes drifted shut and peace filled her.

Now she didn't need to find freedom alone.

CHAPTER *Four*

Angry voices woke her. Startled, Abby sat up. Her head scarf, which she'd forgotten to take off, hung askew. She pushed it from her eyes, noticing the morning sun streaming in through the bedroom window. She'd over-slept!

Abby leaped from the pallet. She'd have to be quick or Mamie would whack her with the stirring spoon. Using Miss Julia's mirror, she rewound her scarf. For a moment, she studied her face in the cloudy glass. *Does Mama look like me?* she wondered. *Big-eyed and stick skinny?*

The voices grew louder, drawing Abby to the window. She peered out. A group of field hands stood on the front lawn. Abby could see the tops of their hats. Why weren't they in the fields?

Then she remembered: They didn't have to toil anymore. They were free!

"Why are you still here?" she wanted to call down to them. "Why ain you on the road to freedom?" But she hushed when she heard Mistress's voice coming from below.

Too curious to keep still, Abby flew down the slave stairway and into the parlor. Through the glass of the arched window she could see the front porch. Mistress stood on the top step. Master stood behind her, leaning heavily on his crutch as if his leg pained him. Uncle Zee stood at the bottom of the steps, his slouch hat in his hand, the field hands scattered behind him. He was addressing Mistress, his voice booming like Preacher's when he smote the listeners with their sins.

"You had no right to keep freedom from us," Uncle Zee was saying. "No right to keep us workin' in the fields." Behind him, the others muttered their assent.

Someone touched Abby on the shoulder and she spun around. It was Pap. Tissie and Mamie were beside him, their eyes wide with curiosity. Pap put a finger to his lips then nodded toward the porch, and Abby turned back to listen.

"I realize I was wrong." Mistress sounded flustered. "I wanted to wait until planting was done to tell you the war was over. I was afraid you'd leave, and we *need* this crop. Don't you see? We need the corn, hemp, and wheat to survive. We need each other to keep the plantation—our home—alive and running."

Uncle Zee shook his head. "No, Mistress Hammond. This ain our home. This *your* home. Your crop. That mean you need *us* to survive. We doan need you."

Many hats bobbed in agreement. Before leaving for the war, Master had placed Uncle Zee in charge of running the farm, and most of the field hands respected him.

"That's not true. We need each other!" Mistress insisted shrilly. Abby saw her glance beseechingly at her husband as if hoping for support, but Master was gazing up at the porch columns as if the truth was in the swallows' nests.

Mistress turned back to the waiting men. "I also didn't tell because I was trying to protect you. The war may be over, but the roads and towns are swarming with angry men who claim to be upholding the law. They're stopping all coloreds on the road, calling them vagrants."

"They sound like patrollers," Uncle Zee said. "Only now we are free. And a free man has rights."

"Not when he meets a mob in the dark," Mistress replied, and Abby heard murmurs of distress.

Then someone yelled from behind Zee. "How we

know you tellin' the truth when you lie to us 'bout bein' free!"

Mistress wrung her hands. "I-I realize you may not believe me. However, it *is* the truth. The roads and towns aren't safe. Please. Listen, if you'll stay, Mister Hammond will pay you with a share of the crop."

Abby's eyes widened. *Mister* Hammond. Was that his new name?

"You can continue to stay in your cabins," Mistress continued. "Mister Hammond will work up a contract for each family."

Amazed at the words coming from Mistress, Abby pressed her fingers to her mouth. Master and Mistress had always treated their slaves kindly. But never once had she heard them say *pay*, *shares*, or *contract*. Those were true words of freedom!

Uncle Zee turned to speak with the other workers, his voice low. When he faced Mistress again, his face was solemn. "Some wants to leave. Some wants to pray on this."

"That's fair," Mistress said. "In the meantime, Master . . . I mean *Mister* Hammond will draw up a contract for those who wish to stay. It will include food, clothing, a garden and cabin for each family, *and* a share of the crop," she added quickly as if to sweeten the minds of the disbanding men.

Whirling around, Abby hugged Pap. "Did you hear that? We doan have a master no more. The Lord *was* listenin'!"

Pap's eyes glistened. "I never thought I'd see the day."

Tissie began to cry into her apron. "Now my Cyril kin *never* be taken from me. I needs to find my babe and tell him the good news," she added, hurrying from the room.

Only Mamie's eyes were dry. Abby gave her an anxious look. "Doan you see what this means, Mamie? We can leave Hammond House. We can look for your daughter—my Mama."

"Who be this '*we*' you talkin' 'bout?" Mamie asked.

"You, me, and Pap!"

"No Ma'am." Mamie shook her head. "Me and Pap, this our home. 'Sides, we too old to be chasin' fool dreams."

Abby stared at her, speechless. "You doan want your own house?"

Mamie barked with laughter. "Chile, you think some white person gonna give us a house like it Christmas? 'Sides, we gots a room, a garden, and a place to die right here."

"Then I'll go alone!" Abby stomped her bare foot. "This ain my home! My home is with my Mama!"

"An where you gonna start lookin' for your Ma?"

Mamie snapped. "What you gonna use for food and money? What you gonna do when those patrollers ketch you? You— a girl chile wid no sense!"

Blood rushed to Abby's face. "I ain a girl no more! I 'most fourteen! And I kin read and write as good as any white chile!"

Grabbing Abby by the shoulders, Mamie shook her like a dirty rug. "Readin' and writin' ain goin' to keep the patrollers from doin' ugly things to you," she spat. "Or help you survive in a city of white faces. Jest git that fool notion out of your head. As long as I live, Abby Joyner, this be your home!"

"Then I hope you die!" Abby blurted. Instantly she gasped at the horror of her words. Then she flinched, expecting the blow she deserved, but Mamie only dropped her hands from her shoulders, gave her a sorrowful look, and shuffled from the room.

"Mamie, I didn't mean. . . ." Abby started to go after her, but Pap caught her arm. "Let your grandma go, chile. You two need some coolin' off 'fore you apologize."

Tears sprang into Abby's eyes. "Oh, Pap, I didn't mean to say it. I jest git so furious with her. Why's Mamie so stubborn 'bout freedom? Why won't she talk to me 'bout my Mama?"

Pap shrugged. "You know I ain your blood grandpa, chile, so I doan know the story of your Mama." Abby had never known her real grandpa, Henry Joyner, who had died long before she was born. Three years before the war, Master had brought Elisha Garvey, no longer young but full of knowledge, to the farm to help turn the orchards into the finest in Virginia. Mamie had fixed Elisha her apple dumplings, Abby had fixed him with her loving smile, and he'd been her Pap ever since.

"What happened to your Mama came long before me," Pap continued. "And Mamie keep the story tight inside."

"That ain right," Abby protested. "I deserves to know 'bout my own Mama!"

Pap sighed. "Maybe it the only way your grandma survives the pain of losin' her."

"Then she only thinkin' 'bout *her* pain. What 'bout mine?"

"Maybe she thinkin' of your pain too, chile." Pap touched her cheek. "Ever think of that?"

"Never," Abby declared. "I think Mamie's a selfish, stubborn ol' woman only thinkin' 'bout herself. She afraid of findin' her own chile, much less freedom."

Pap chuckled. "An maybe *you* a selfish, stubborn chile only thinkin' 'bout *your*self. Your grandma and me ain young no more. Others will leave to find freedom, but Mamie's right—Hammond House is where we'll die. Mamie wants to be buried in the cemetery beside your Pa."

"Oh, oh, *hog swill*." Frustrated, Abby flounced from the parlor. As soon as she was out of Pap's sight, she tore from the Big House. Bare feet pounding, she headed down the hill toward the quarters. Mamie may not be ready to embrace freedom, but Abby knew the field slaves would be rejoicing.

Abby was right. The quarters hummed like springtime after a long winter. Children ran from cabin to cabin laughing. Women hollered to each other from the front stoops. A group of men clustered under the big oak. When Abby passed by them, she slowed to hear their talk. Words flew from their mouths so fast she couldn't catch them all, but she heard "leavin', stayin', north, south, contract, land."

Abby found Uncle Zee rocking on his porch, whittling a stick as if he had all the time in the world.

"What you waitin' for, Uncle Zee?" she asked.

"I's waitin' to see if the hands gonna stay or go. Figure it'll take them a day or two of chewin' on it."

"Why ain *you* packin'?"

"To go where, Miss Abby?"

"To find freedom!"

"And where that be?"

"It's—" Abby caught herself, and Zee chuckled.

Abby plopped her fists on her hips. "I doan know for sure," she admitted tartly. "What I do know is that it ain here in these cabins. It's north." She waved her hand down the lane. "Or in Charlottesville with my *Mama*." She gave Zee a sly look. He'd been living on Hammond Plantation as long as she could remember, but his face was always closed on the subject of her Mama.

"Chile, I bin to Charlottesville," he said instead. "It a city where black and white will steal you blind faster than you kin say 'freedom.'"

"Well, then I'll make my way to New York City."

Throwing back his head, Zee laughed heartily. "And what do you know of New York City?"

"I seen it in pictures."

"Oh, I see. *Pictures*. And how you gettin' there?"

"A train. I seen pictures of those, too."

"An' where you gettin' train fare?"

"I—I kin earn it."

"Doin' what?"

"I kin cook and sew and—"

Uncle Zee crooked one brow. "You be doin' that now for Master and Mistress. Only they be good to you. Youngun, you have no idea of the meanness in this world." He shook his head, his expression melancholy. Abby knew Zee had suffered mightily at the hand of his first master. He'd told chilling tales of slaves hung by their thumbs or tied down to blister in the burning sun.

"You sound just like Tissie," Abby declared in frustration.

He smiled. "Tissie and me have the same mind."

"Oh, oh, *possum tails!*" Furious at Zee, Abby spun to find someone who *would* rejoice with her. She found Rafe and his wife Sally in their cabin tossing their belongings onto their bed quilt. Their two young children, Patsey and Samuel, were hanging onto Sally's skirts. A basket sat on a chair. It was filled with a sack of corn meal, paper-wrapped bacon, and a passel of withered sweet potatoes from last year's harvest.

When the two little ones saw Abby, they toddled over calling "Babby!" and pressed their cheeks into her knees.

Abby patted the tops of their heads. "You all leavin'?"

Rafe nodded. "I doan wants to work Master's land one more day. I wants my own land. My own plow."

And how will you buy it? Zee would ask, but not she. "Can I go with you?"

Rafe nodded. "We kin use a fine girl like you to cook and scrub and watch the babies all day while Sally and I work our fields."

Cook? Scrub? Abby's brows shot up. She gazed down at Patsey and Sam with their grimy faces and snotty noses. The two were fun to play with on Sunday after Mistress read the scriptures, but all day?

"Uh, which way you goin'?" she asked.

"Over the mountain to the Valley. I hear the land mighty sweet there."

"Oh, well. That's the wrong way. I want to go to Charlottesville."

"Fine wid us." Rafe threw a tin pot onto the quilt. Sally added a ladle and wooden spoon, and her husband bundled it all into a sack and tied the ends with rope.

Abby began to back out the door. "Stop by the kitchen 'fore you leave. Mamie sure to give you enough victuals to last a few days."

"We aim to." Rafe threw the quilt sack over one shoulder and hoisted Patsey to the other. Sally held Sam with one hand and picked up the basket. She glanced once around the cabin, and Abby thought she saw the shine of tears. But then Sally hurried out the door after her husband.

Abby stood on the stoop and watched them go. Heads high, they strode down the lane, the first to leave, while the others called goodbye.

Abby waved, but what she really wanted to do was trot alongside and ask how it felt to leave without a pass. To leave without permission from Zee or Mistress. To leave because *you jest plain want to leave!*

She was burning to find out. Spinning around, she ran to Malinda's cabin. She reckoned Malinda and her sons, Buck and Mitchell, would be next to go, and if she recalled right, Malinda had family in Charlottesville.

When she burst into the cabin, Malinda was throwing bowls, candles, and clothes willy-nilly into a basket.

"You leavin'?" Abby asked excitedly.

"Yes, I is."

"Goin' to Charlottesville?"

"Yes, I is."

"Buck and Mitchell goin' too?"

"No, dey ain't. Dey stayin' here and workin' for a share of de crop and den joinin' me after harvest."

"Can I come with you?" Abby tagged after the older woman, who began to strip the straw mattress of its blanket. "I can carry your basket."

Without pausing, Malinda nodded. "Yes, you kin. My sister Weezy and her four chillens live in a room behind the tavern. One more sharin' deir bed doan matter."

Abby gulped. *Five in a bed?* She pictured Julia's spacious room, her own pallet and trunk neatly arranged in the corner by the precious books.

"Weezy need help servin' in the tavern." Malinda looked Abby up and down with an appraising eye. "She kin use a strong, comely girl like you."

"Oh, a tavern!" Abby edged toward the cabin door. "I doubts Mamie and the Lord allow me to serve liquor. Thank you for your kind offer, Malinda, and may Jesus watch over you on your journey," she added as she rushed out the door, her head pounding. The thought of leaving Mamie, Pap and her own bed was filling her with an unexpected ache.

In front of the cabin the group of field slaves had broken up. Johnson, a gangly boy about four years older than Abby, called out, "Mornin' Miss Abby." He touched the brim of his hat. "I hear you ready to find freedom. Jump the broom wid me and we find it together."

Startled, Abby could only stare at him. *Johnson's invitin' me to marry him!* The idea made her mouth go dry, and she croaked like a frog when she replied, "Uh-h-h, no thank you, Mister Johnson. I be a peck too young to marry."

His gaze swept from her head to her toes, and Abby felt heat rise up her neck when he grinned and said, "Well, Miss Abby, you might be skinny as a corn stalk but I believe you jest right for me."

The other men hooted with laughter. Flushing mightily, Abby turned and ran from the cabins. As she raced up the path, a sob rose in her throat.

Mamie was right. She *was* just a girl chile—too foolish to find freedom on her own, too young to leave her grandma's arms.

But if I don't set off, I'll never find my Mama! Abby thought sorrowfully, and the disappointment felt as heavy as the chains of slavery.

* * *

CHAPTER *Five*

Pap found her huddled in a corner of the cool, empty springhouse. "There, there," he said, patting her shoulder soothingly. "Tell your ol' Pap what's ailin' you."

Sitting up, Abby wiped her cheeks on her apron. "Freedom what's ailin' me," she choked out. "Rafe, Sally, Malinda—they all on their way to findin' it. Only I'm too scared to leave you and Mamie."

"An' that so bad?" he asked gently.

"It mean I woan *never* find my Mama!"

Pap squatted beside her, his knees cracking. "Abby, your grandma love you more than life. If you left, she wither and die like a plucked flower. Jest be patient with her instead of firin' questions like hailstones, and I 'spect she tell you 'bout your Mama."

Abby lowered the apron. "But she never tol' me before. Why would she now?"

"Maybe she know it's time you heard. And chile," he gave her a searching look, "freedom doan have to mean settin' out t. 'he city of Charlottesville. Maybe some folk find it right here at Hammond Plantation."

Abby pondered Pap's words, and then, since she hated to fret longer than a good cry, she scrambled to her feet. "I hope you're right."

"You ever know'd your Pap to be wrong?" he teased. "Now help me up, girl."

She pulled him snapping and creaking to his feet. He rubbed his back and groaned. "See why this ol' man cain't walk the roads to Charlottesville?"

Abby laughed. "Freedom to you mean a feather bed."

"Um um." His eyes lighted as he limped from the springhouse. "Now there's a pleasant thought."

Linking her arm with Pap's, Abby helped him up the path to the kitchen. She could hear Mamie clattering pots and pans.

"Sounds like she's 'bout to tear the kitchen down," she whispered to Pap.

"Or she whackin' rats with the skillet," he whispered back, and they both giggled. Stopping at the door, he gave her a nudge. "Now you go apologize."

"Yes suh." Hesitantly, Abby stepped through the doorway. As she watched Mamie hobble to the fireplace, her body crippled from years of hard work, Abby felt a pang. How could she have expected her grandma to up and leave Hammond House?

Picking up tongs, Mamie poked in the ashes. "Let me help you take the taters from the hot coals," Abby called as she rushed across the kitchen floor.

Mamie slowly straightened, and Abby gave her a hug. Her grandma's arms stole around her, and for a moment they swayed into each other. Then, just as quickly, Mamie pushed her away and handed her the tongs. "Best get them taters 'fore dey burn. Ain no meat for supper 'cept a slab of old salt pork."

"Maybe Uncle Zee trap a possum," Abby said as she leaned over the hearth, the heat scalding the hairs straying from her head scarf. "Least then the quarters have a celebration."

Mamie chuckled. "Dem slaves need no reason to celebrate."

"They ain slaves no more, Grandma," Abby pointed out. "They *free* men now. Rafe and Sally and Malinda took off already."

Mamie crossed her arms on her bosom. "And where dey takin' off to like deir feet on fire?"

Abby felt impatience growing in her chest like

weeds. It was one thing for Mamie not to want freedom. But why couldn't she understand that others wanted to drink it like Master's fine brandy?

She kept her tongue in check. "Rafe and Sally headed for the Valley. Malinda's goin' to her sister's in *Charlottesville*." Abby said the name of the town loudly, hoping to see some sign in Mamie's eyes. But her grandma only picked up a head of cabbage, brown and moldy from being buried in the root cellar, and sliced it in half with a knife.

Abby sighed. So much for Mamie being eager to talk about her Mama.

"Missus better tell Zee and the hands to butcher a hog soon," Mamie said. "Or we all look like broom poles 'fore the new harvest come in."

"Maybe he'll butcher one so we can *all* celebrate," Abby suggested.

Mamie humphed. "Woan be no celebration in the Big House. Missus bin church quiet since dis mornin'."

"Doan feel sorry for Mistress," Abby retorted, plucking the last potato from the powdery ashes. "Us slaves bin fetchin' and washin' for her for too long."

"Missus had her share of hurt these last years too, Miss Uppity." Mamie waved the knife at her. "Her husband come home from the war half dead, and she lost her only chile."

"At least she know where *her* chile is," Abby declared.

But Mamie only set her jaw and gave the cabbage another whack.

More stubborn than Toby! Frustration pricked Abby, and she knew she had to get away from the stifling kitchen and her ornery grandma.

"How 'bout I pick some wild greens to cook with the pork and cabbage?" she offered as she hung the tongs on the hook.

"Um um. Fresh greens sound tasty. Git Cyril to help. He lookin' for guinea eggs in the orchard."

"Yes um." Abby grabbed a basket and dashed out the kitchen door. Picking up her skirt with one hand, she raced through the garden. In the orchard she breathed in deeply. The spring air was sweet with the scent of apple and peach blossoms.

When Pap came to the plantation Master Hammond had carefully listened to his new slave's advice. Prune the trees high, then pasture the stock in the orchard, Pap had said. The cattle will eat the diseased fruit, the chickens will eat the bugs, and the manure will feed the trees. For a while the orchards had flourished, but since the war, they'd been poorly tended. The cattle were gone, the chickens had scattered, the branches needed pruning, and fireblight had plagued last summer's crop.

Reaching up Abby plucked a cluster of blossoms and

tucked it behind one ear. Then she dropped the basket and twirled in a circle, music from long ago parties filling her head.

Gone was the task of picking greens. The fresh air had stolen her foul mood. Maybe she wouldn't set out on the road to Charlottesville. Maybe Mamie wouldn't talk about long ago and she'd have to put off finding her Mama. But she was still free, and if her heart chose to dance in the orchard, *no* one was going to tell her *she couldn't!*

Then a powerful thought struck Abby and she collapsed in the weeds, her head dizzy with a new possibility. *Even if I'm tethered to Hammond House, Mama is free. And right now, somewhere on the road to Tomasford, she could be comin' for me!*

❋ ❋ ❋

"Oh, Pap, I can see Mama now," Abby said excitedly as she followed him through the orchard. It was three days after freedom, and they were hunting for wild honey, the plantation's bee hives having long been destroyed. "She wearin' a bonnet and high steppin' toward Hammond House like one of Mister's carriage horses. And in her hand she holdin' a picture of me when I was a babe."

Stopping, Pap brought a finger to his lips. Abby carried a tin bucket in case they happened upon early huckleberries. Pap carried a forked stick in case they happened upon copperheads. "Quiet, chile," he whispered. "Your prattlin' is drownin' out the bees."

Abby hushed, the thought of sweet honey almost as powerful as the dream of her Mama. Days ago, Pap had lured a dozen bees into his bait box. This morning, when the wind was still, he'd let half of them go in the blooms. Now he and Abby were going to follow one back to the hive.

Keen as a hungry bear, Pap gazed intently at a peach tree. Several bees hummed around the blossoms. One landed, feasted, and then flew into the air. It circled several times before zooming away.

Pap signaled Abby to chase after it. Sprinting ahead, she kept her eyes on the bee, which, true to nature, would fly in a straight line back to its home. She lost sight of it in the thicket beyond the orchard.

Frustrated, she flapped her skirt. "Oh, *stink bug!* My mouth was waterin' for that honey."

"Doan fret, chile," Pap called as he hobbled to catch up. "I got a bead on its path. We'll let the last of the bees loose and see if they go in the same direction." One by one, Pap let out the rest of the bees. Several flew into the blossoms. One set out along the same path as the first bee.

"We follow that one," Pap said. "Bee tree shouldn't be more than two or so miles ahead."

Abby set off after it, but her skirt got hung up on the briars, and the bee quickly disappeared in the scrub.

"Doan worry. I gots the beeline in my head." Pap gestured for Abby to move closer. "Let me show you the secret of trackin' bees. When I's gone, you be the one keepin' the Big House in honey."

"Doan you talk like that, Pap." Abby shushed him. "You be here forever. Like one of them spirits you always talkin' 'bout."

Pap drew her in front of him. Raising one hand, he pointed to a cedar tree. "See that cedar tree yonder, the locust beyond it, and the dogwood smack dab beyond the locust?"

Abby nodded. "Now squint one eye and pretend there a rope stretched taut from tree to tree to tree. That's the line dose bees travelin'. We hike to the cedar then use the locust and dogwood to find our next line." He chuckled. "We ain as smart as dose bees but we more determined. Follow their path 'til we hear buzzin'."

Slipping a hatchet from his homemade sheath, Pap made a notch on the cedar and then on the locust and dogwood when they reached them. For an hour they traveled slowly uphill from tree to tree, marking each with a notch. They walked through dark woods and on sunny hillsides, sometimes losing the line. Then they doubled back to a notch and started over until finally

Pap stopped, cocked his head, and said, "Listen, gal."

Abby held her breath. Her ears picked out the mur-
mur of the wind, the chatter of a squirrel, and the call
of the crows. "Pap, I doan . . ."

He nudged her. "Listen like a bee."

Closing her eyes, Abby held still, and then she heard
a noise like water rushing over rocks.

"That's the hum of bees," Pap said. "They singin' to
you. 'Abby, Abby come to me. Take sweet honey from
this tree.'"

Abby giggled. "You joshin' me, Pap." Tipping her
head, she moved in a circle, trying to locate the hive.
Pap halted her twirling and pointed to a tree, its gnarled
limbs bare of spring leaves. About five feet up the trunk,
Abby spotted several bees darting in and out of a small
hole.

"Bees like them old, hollow gum trees," Pap said.

"If the honey's inside, how are we gettin' it out?"

"That be Pap's secret." He tapped his temple with one
finger. "One thing I will tell you—always hunt honey in
spring when the bees ain't hungry 'cause a hungry bee is
a mean bee. I pass this on to you gal 'cause when I gone,
you be the honey hunter."

Abby whacked him on the arm. "You quit talkin' like
that," she snapped. "I doan want the Lord hearin' you
and totin' you off to Heaven."

"Chile." Pap smiled dreamily. "I done lived a long time. Now that I've seen freedom I'm 'most ready to see Heaven."

"No!" Abby grasped Pap's arm, wanting to shake the old man. Her Mama had left. Miss Julia had left. How dare he even think of leaving! "*No*, Pap. You ain never going to leave Mamie and me," she said fiercely. "*Never!*"

Pap shook his head. "Never be a long time, Abby. Now we best head back 'fore it gets dark."

"What about our honey?"

"We marked the trail. Tomorrow we'll have honey." He patted Abby's cheek. "Pap promises."

✳ ✳ ✳

Hands clasped primly, Abby stood with Mamie and Pap before Mistress, who was seated at her desk. It was five days after freedom, and Mistress had summoned them to the parlor.

"This is a legal contract," Mistress explained as she blotted the ink on the paper in front of her. "*Abby* can read it to you," she added, sharp-tongued. "And *this* time she has my permission."

Abby's stomach roiled like soup over a hot fire. Was Mistress finally going to punish her for spilling the secret of freedom? But Mistress only blew on the ink and handed the paper to her.

"Mister Hammond and I want to be fair," she continued

in a clear voice. Abby noticed her cheeks were rouged and her hair neatly coiled as if presenting *wages* and *shares* to coloreds took all her dignity. "However, we have naught to give until crops are harvested."

"Beggin' your pardon, Missus," Mamie said just as clearly. "Me and Pap 'spect to stay on, only we doan want no share of the harvest."

Mamie gave Pap a shy look. Ducking his head, he said, "Mamie and me want a proper bed with four posts and a feather mattress."

"I knowed the farm is poorly, but perhaps you could give us your silver tea set in exchange for work," Mamie suggested. "No call for fancy tea parties dese days."

Abby's jaw dropped at her grandma's boldness. She'd been wrong about Mamie and Pap. The two must have been thinking on freedom for days!

Abby wondered if Mistress would be indignant at their demand, but she knit her forehead as if pondering the idea. "I was going to use the tea service to barter for another mule," she finally said. "We'll need a team for the harvest."

Mamie folded her arms across her bosom. "And who gonna pickle, salt, preserve, and bake that harvest?" she asked pertly. "Or you plannin' on teachin' dat new mule to cook?"

Abby smothered a grin.

"If me and Pap use dat tea service to git us a feather bed, we sleep so good at night we work as hard as two mules."

Mistress worried her lip. "Yes, I see the sense in your proposition." Taking the contract from Abby, she dipped the pen in the ink and began to write.

"I 'spect the tea service be fair wages, Missus," Mamie replied. "As long as dat contract also say we have a roof over our heads and food in our stomachs."

"Why, of course."

"Fo' as long as Pap and me live," Mamie added firmly. "No turnin' us out when we's too old to work."

"I wouldn't think of it." Mistress lifted her pen. "And Abby, what would you like in exchange for work?"

Speechless, Abby only stared at Mistress. No one had ever asked her such a question in her life!

"Abby wants to continue her learnin'," Mamie answered, much to Abby's amazement. It was the first time her grandma had deemed reading and writing important. "Dat mean each day she spend time readin' and writin'. I doan want her slavin' her whole life."

"I'll be pleased to teach her myself."

Mamie tapped the paper with a steely finger. "You writes all dat on de contract."

"Of course." Mistress bent over the paper again before handing Abby the contract. Abby reddened, knowing it would take her a while to cipher all the words, but her grandma settled herself on the settee and said, "Take your time, chile."

Abby read aloud while Mamie sang out a hearty "Amen" after each line of the contract. When she was finished reading, Pap cleared his throat. "Abby, that be most beautiful readin'," he said. Turning to Mistress he bowed. "Thank you," he told her. "We be most reverent and faithful workers."

"And thank you for staying on, Elisha. You are sorely needed. If you'll each sign your names on these lines."

"I'll sign," Abby said quickly, knowing her grandma had never even held a pen.

"I kin make my own mark." Pap picked up the pen and wrote a clear E and G. "That stand for me, Elisha Garvey, free man."

Abby signed her and Mamie's names with a flourish. Then she handed everything to Mistress who stood and said, "I'm glad we came to an agreement. I know it will take years of hard work, but with your help, Mister Hammond and I hope to make Hammond Plantation prosperous again. Now, if there's nothing else to discuss . . . Mamie, can we expect supper at noon?"

"You can 'spect supper," Mamie replied. "Jest doan 'spect much. Root cellar bare, and de kitchen garden sproutin', but it a sight too early for greens or peas. Now if Zee were to butcher a hog . . ."

Mistress laid a finger against her cheek. "If Zee butchers a hog this early, we may not have enough provisions for winter."

Pap cleared his throat again. "Might I make a suggestion?"

"Please do." Mistress seemed relieved.

"Mas—*Mis*ter Hammond ain shot his rifle since he came home," Pap said. "Let Zee and Buck use it to hunt. Give them three days and they'll have enough game for a week."

"My." Mistress placed her hand on her throat. "I don't know if Mister Hammond would allow someone else to shoot his rifle, and if Zee is hunting, who will keep the hands working in the fields?"

"Beggin' your pardon, but if the hands sign a contract, they woan need a boss," Pap said. "They be workin' for themselves. An as for the matter of the rifle," he lowered his voice, "I doan believe Mister Hammond will knowed it's gone."

Mistress stood so abruptly that Abby stumbled backward. "Mister Hammond will soon be well and in charge," she stated. "I'm sure of it. However, until his health is better, the first order is for the occupants of this farm to survive. I suppose I have no other choice than to let Zee and Buck hunt. And Elisha, what you say about the workers may be true, but until I know for sure that they won't need a firm hand, I'm placing you in charge. Soon the wheat will need to be harvested and the corn seed planted."

"Yes, Ma'am."

"Now please see to your chores."

Mamie humphed. "You doan need to order us, Missus."

A flush rose up Mistress's neck. "You're right. I'm—" She stopped, a look of confusion crossing her face.

Sorry? Is Mistress about to apologize to a colored woman?

"Now, if there's nothing else to discuss, you'll excuse me," Mistress said. "I need to show these contracts to Mister Hammond. If he's up to it. He woke this morning feeling poorly."

When Mamie and Pap left, Abby lingered behind. "Pardon, Ma'am, there is one more thing I'd like to discuss."

"Yes?"

"My Mama," she said quickly. "I woan never be free unless I knowed what happened to her."

Lacing her fingers together, Abby held them out as if in prayer. "Please, Mistress, you knew her. You knew my Mama. Is she still in Virginy? Is she livin' in Charlottesville? Is she comin' for me now that I'm free?"

Mistress's face blanched. "Your-r-r . . . your . . . mama?" she gasped. Then her eyes rolled up in her head, and she crumpled in a heap at Abby's feet.

CHAPTER *Six*

Abby screamed in horror. *I've killed Mistress!*

"Mamie! Pap!" She raced from the parlor as if snakes were after her. Pap and Mamie were halfway down the hall. When they heard Abby scream, they turned.

"I killed Mistress!" Abby cried. "I'll be hung for sure!"

Pushing past Abby, Pap limped back into the parlor. Mamie took Abby by the upper arms. "What you talkin' 'bout, chile?"

Abby began to sob. "I asked Mistress about Mama. I jest wanted to know—"

Mamie reared back. "You asked her *what?*"

"'Bout Mama," she wailed.

Mamie's eyes darkened to coals. "You had no call to bring up your mama to Missus," she said, and dropping her hands as if disgusted, she hurried after Pap.

With a moan, Abby shrank against the wall, tears streaming down her cheeks. *What have I done? Free only five days and I've killed my Mistress! A woman who mostly treated me kindly!*

Tissie came running down the hall. "What the devil goin' on? I heard you screamin' all the way in the laundry!"

Sobbing too hard to reply, Abby gestured toward the parlor.

Tissie's gaze flew to the doorway. "No, ma'am, I ain goin' in dere alone. No tellin' what I find." Taking Abby's hand, Tissie tugged her down the hall and into the parlor with her.

Pap was on one knee, fanning Mistress's face. Mamie was bent over, slapping her cheeks. When she spied Tissie, she said, "Git a cool rag. Missus plum fainted."

"Fainted-d-d?" Abby stammered. "She ain dead?"

Mamie gave her a cross look. "No thanks to you and your fool pesterin'. If I hear one mo' word 'bout your mama, I lock you in the root cellar. Now quit bawlin' and git a pillow."

Abby ran into the hall and without thinking leaped up the spiral staircase. Mister Hammond stood at the top, his shirt hanging open, a disoriented expression on his face.

"My God, the Yankees are slaughtering my men!" he

cried when he saw Abby. "Listen to their screams! We've got to fall back! Sergeant!" he hollered down the stairs as he teetered unsteadily on his crutch. "Give the order to fall back!"

"No, Mister." Abby clutched his arm, trying to keep him from falling down the steps. "It was me screamin.' *Abby*." Staring intently into his face, she tried to get him to focus on her, and she saw the fever in his bloodshot eyes.

"The war over, Mister Hammond," she said gently. "You lost your leg. Now you home and *sick*. Come back to bed."

His face fell slack. Nodding, he licked his parched lips and, leaning on Abby, made his way into his darkened bedroom.

Abby wrinkled her nose, the stench hitting her when she walked in. The bedcovers on Mister's massive oak bed were soaked with sweat. Since Mamie couldn't climb the stairs anymore, Mistress had been caring for Mister's stump, and Abby smelled the rot of gangrene.

With a groan, Mister dropped his crutch and fell onto the rumpled spread. Careful not to touch his bandages, Abby helped him swing his legs onto the mattress. Then she wrung her hands.

Oh, nothing is right! She wanted to moan out loud. Freedom was supposed to be finding her Mama, not caring for the sick. Freedom was supposed to be sweet as honey, not sour as fever. "I needs to git a pillow for Mistress," Abby said to Mister, although he seemed beyond caring. "Then I be right back."

Grabbing a pillow off Miss Julia's bed, Abby raced downstairs. Pap was still fanning, Mamie still patting, and Tissie was pressing a cool rag on Mistress's brow. Abby bent to put the pillow under Mistress's head.

Mamie swatted her hand. "Under her feet. We need the life flowin' back in her head."

"Yes 'um." As Abby lifted Mistress's feet by each heel, she noted the worn soles of her shoes and the mends in her stockings. It wasn't so long ago when Mistress had dressed in the fanciest silks and satins and Master had worn the finest breeches and boots. The war had made everyone raggedy.

Mistress moaned. Tipping her chin up, she asked, "What happened? Why am I on the floor?" Abby gave a relieved sigh. Mistress wasn't dead—only Abby's dream of finding out about her Mama was.

Pap and Tissie helped Mistress to the settee.

"Mamie," Abby whispered to her grandma. "Mister Hammond's feverish. It smells like his stump is bad. What we goin' to do?"

"We goin' to care for him," Mamie whispered back. Then she took Mistress's hand. "Tissie make you some tea, Missus. Pap get you a blanket. You rest now."

Mistress shook her head weakly. "No time. I must finish the contracts so the hands will work, and there's no food in the larder and . . . and . . . John! I have to tend to him." Panicking, she tried to rise. Mamie pressed her down.

"Right now, you leave Mista Hammond to me, Abby, and the Lord," Mamie told her. "You'll do him no good as poorly as you is. Do I have your promise?"

Tears welled in Mistress's eyes. "Just until I rest."

"Come, chile." Mamie took Abby's arm. "We got work to do. We need boilin' water and an old sheet for bandages," she instructed as she propelled Abby toward the kitchen. "An' clean sheets off the line. As you makin' up Mista's bed, you throw open the winders and let the sunshine chase the sick out of dat room.

"Cyril!" Mamie bellowed without breaking stride. "Abby needs help with Mista Hammond's bed!"

Breaking free of Mamie's iron grip, Abby hurried from the kitchen to the laundry. When she rounded the corner, she almost fell over Cyril, who was crouched beside a stack of wood. "What are you doin'?"

"Hidin' from your grandma. I ain goin' to work today. I's goin' fishin' with Lanny."

"Oh, no you ain't." Abby hauled him to his feet. "You helpin' me with Mister. He powerful sick."

Cyril shook her off. "No I ain't," he declared. "You tol' me when I's free I doan have to work, and I ain't."

"I was foolish for sayin' that." Abby shook her finger in his face. "You listen here, Cyril. Freedom means workin' so no one starve. Freedom means carin' for all so no one die."

"Who care if Mister die?" Cyril taunted.

"I care. And so should you unless you wants to leave Hammond House forever."

"Now that I's free I kin leaves whenever I wants!" Cyril boasted.

"And where you go?" she asked him, sounding like Uncle Zee.

"To my Pa."

Rolling her eyes, Abby hurried to the wash line, Cyril tagging on her heels. "And what if your Pa doan want you?" she asked as she yanked the clean sheets off the line.

"Why wouldn't he want me?"

Abby whirled, sheets in her arms, and glowered down at him. "'Cause you jest a lazy boy who doan care nothin' 'bout others."

Cyril dragged a toe in the dirt. "I do too care 'bout others," he said sullenly.

Abby handed him the sheets. "Good, then carry these up to Mister's bedroom. And doan mind his ravin' 'bout the war. He's burnin' up with fever."

"All right, but *den* I go fishin'."

Abby ruffled his springy hair. "*Then* you can go fishin', but only if you catch a mess for dinner."

Abby watched Cyril run down the path and into the Big House, the sheets flying from his arms like wings. *Wish I could fly away,* Abby thought wistfully. *Fly from all these problems.*

Heavy hearted, she plucked a clean rag from the line. "Though it seems like I'm not the only one confused 'bout freedom," she muttered as she tore it into strips for bandages.

Mistress didn't know how to treat the slaves.

Slaves didn't know how to talk to Mistress.

No one knew how to act.

And even worse, she'd never again be able to ask Mistress about her Mama. Gathering the torn strips, Abby sighed as she headed to the kitchen thinking that life had gotten mighty jangled-up.

✳ ✳ ✳

Abby poked her head through the doorway of Mister Hammond's bedroom. It was night, seven days since freedom, and a lone candle flickered from the side table. Abby could make out Mistress's dark form in the rocker by the bed. Mister was a lump under the quilt. The room had been aired and wiped down daily, but

Abby could tell by the fetid air that his stump still wasn't healing.

"Mistress," Abby called in a low voice. "Mamie said you need to come down to eat. This morning, Zee shot several rabbits and there's stew cookin' over the fire."

"Tell Mamie I have no appetite."

"No Ma'am. I cain't tell her that. She chase me back up the stairs until you come down. She say you cain't nurse your husband if you ain't strong."

The rocker stilled. "I suppose she's right."

Abby tiptoed into the room. "I'll take care of him."

"Thank you." Rising, Mistress took a folded rag off her husband's forehead and dipped it into a pan of water on the table. "One minute he's burning up. One minute he's shivering," she said. "I'm at a loss."

Abby bit her tongue. Once before she'd mentioned Mamie's healing ways with wild plants, roots, and spells. Mistress had hushed her, saying that an educated woman must have faith in modern medicine.

"Abby, did you know that I was born in the North?" Mistress asked as she wrung the water from the cloth.

Abby pricked her ears at the news. "No, Ma'am."

"In Baltimore, Maryland. My father and mother moved south to Staunton, Virginia, when I was a little older than you are. My father taught at Augusta Female Seminary. That's where I met John, Mister

Hammond. He would ride into town on business. He said he liked the culture—and the ladies—of Staunton better than those in Charlottesville." She smiled as she folded the cloth and lay it back on Mister's forehead.

"What I'm trying to explain is that when I married Mister Hammond, I was naïve about slavery. I only knew what I'd heard in conversation or read in books. When I arrived at the plantation, the reality was a shock. Mister Hammond was born and raised in the South. He assured me that slavery was necessary for the plantation—for the South—to survive. And I believed him and closed my heart to my misgivings."

Abby plucked at her skirt, wondering why Mistress was telling her this.

"When Mister Hammond left to fight in the war, I was frantic," Mistress continued, smoothing the quilt around her husband's quiet form. "I had no idea how to run a house much less an entire farm. John assured me he'd only be gone for a month and that Zee could handle the daily operations. But the month turned into a year, and as the plantation fell down around me, I knew I had to take responsibility. Only I was alone and scared. Scared we'd starve to death. Scared we'd lose the farm. Then Julia died and I was devastated and beyond reason. If I'd listened to my heart, I would have implored

Mister to free you all long ago. And for my lack of con-
viction, I am deeply sorry."

As Abby listened, her throat grew tight. In all her life,
no one except Pap had spoken to her like she was a person with a mind. Especially about something as important as freedom.

"Although an apology certainly won't make up for
years of bondage." Turning, Mistress handed Abby the
pan. "If you will kindly get cool water and watch over
Mister while I eat, I would be most obliged."

"Yes, Ma'am." Taking the pan, Abby backed from the
room. *While Mistress is full of convictions and apologies,
maybe I should ask her about Mama,* she thought. But she
held her tongue and fled down the stairs, afraid that
Mistress might faint again, and Mamie would lock her
in the root cellar.

As she passed through the summer kitchen, Mamie
brandished a ladle. "Where you goin'? You supposed to
be carin' fo' Mista so Missus can get some vittles."

"I'm gettin' fresh water and Mistress will be down
shortly," Abby said. When she hurried back into the Big
House, Mistress was sitting alone in the shadowy dining room.

Abby hurried up the steps and into Mister's room.
She set the pan on the side table next to the ointments
and bottles from Dr. Preston. Wringing out the rag in

the cool water, she laid it on Mister's forehead. His face was hollow beneath his whiskers, his eyes sunken. *Almost like he dead*, Abby thought worriedly. But then she spied the faint rise and fall of his chest under the quilt.

Satisfied that he was still alive, Abby stooped to read the labels on the medicine bottles: laudanum, sulfur, and calomel. Opening the calomel, she sniffed the contents. No wonder Mister was ill. The medicine smelled worse than a privy. Mister needed Mamie's sweet herb tea and cleansing poultices.

Mistress has her mind set on 'modern medicine', Abby reminded herself as she settled in the rocker, content to rest her tired feet. Since signing the contract, she'd been busier than ever. With Mister sick, there'd been no time to dance in the orchard. With Pap in the fields, there'd been no time to return to the honey tree. At night, she was so exhausted she fell in a heap on her pallet, too tired to read more than a page or two. At least the past few days Buck and Zee had shot rabbit, squirrel, and possum, so her stomach was quiet.

A moan from the bed made her start.

Abby rocked forward. Mister's eyes popped open and he stared at the ceiling. His cracked lips began to move as if he was talking and a look of joy filled his face. She tilted her head back, wondering what he saw in his fever. Did he see his comrades lost in the war? Or was it the Lord coming to receive him?

"Julia!" he cried suddenly, and Abby shot from the rocker. "You've finally come! I've waited so long!" Sitting up, the quilt falling to his lap, Mister opened his arms to embrace his daughter.

"Abby, Julia's with us." He stared right at Abby as if he knew who she was, and his arms circled as if cradling someone. "She's come to visit us."

Abby blinked. "Mister? You all right?"

He laughed. "Now that my dear daughter's here everything is fine!" Frowning, he cocked his head and bent lower. "What? What did you say, baby? You have a message for your best friend, Abby?"

Abby's skin grew cold. Mister spoke clearly, but his eyes were glazed and red. It was as if something was inside him, making him talk. Abby thought back to all Pap's stories.

Slowly, she backed away from the bed. "Mister Hammond, is it you talkin'?" she whispered, her heart thumping. "Or is it a haunt?"

"It's Julia. And she has a message for you. About your mother, Lively."

Mama! Abby clapped a hand to her mouth, afraid she might scream. "Li-Li-Lively?" she finally stammered. "Is that my Mama's name?"

Swaying from side to side as if rocking his daughter, Mister began to sing, "Hush little baby don't say a word. Papa's going to buy you a mockingbird."

Abby remembered the song from long ago when Mister would sing Miss Julia to sleep. Before the war had made him a soldier. Before scarlet fever had taken Miss Julia.

"Mister," Abby whispered. "Ask Miss Julia 'bout my Mama. Is she in heaven with her?"

He shook his head. "Lively's on earth, Abby," he replied in a girlish voice. Then suddenly, his expression turned fierce. "No, don't go, baby." He tightened his hold. "Julia! You can't go! I can't lose you again!"

Then just as suddenly, his arms opened in release and he slumped heavily back onto the pillow. Tears coursed down his cheeks. "She's gone," he sobbed over and over, until finally his head fell to one side in exhaustion, and mercifully, his lashes drifted shut.

Abby patted his hand, tears welling in her own eyes. "Oh, Mister Hammond, I'm so sorry she had to leave. But as long as Miss Julia in your heart, she'll always be with you."

Leaning over, she tucked the quilt under his chin. As she bathed his burning forehead, she raised her eyes to the ceiling, searching among the flickering shadows.

Did Miss Julia really visit? Is it she who's haunting Mister? Pap had told her all about spirits returning to earth to finish their business. Mister had been off at war when Miss Julia died. Had her soul been roaming Hammond House like a lost child, waiting for the chance to say goodbye to the father she loved?

Mister grew restless. "Kennedy," he muttered fitfully. "Don't whip him. He's a good man. Gabe's a good man."

Abby stopped bathing him. *Gabe. That was my Pa's name!*

"You must run away. Run, Gabe, *run!*"

Abby held her breath. She knew her Pa had run away. That's when patrollers had shot him. Mamie told her he was running to find freedom. But was he really running to escape a whipping from a man named Kennedy? Had Mister Hammond helped him run? It had all happened fourteen years ago, before Abby was born. So why was Mister rambling on about it now? Was guilt weighing heavily on *his* soul?

"Abby, what's going on?" Mistress hurried into the room carrying a decanter, and Abby jumped away from the bed.

"Um, Mister's hot and restless. I'm trying to cool him, but he's thrashing so."

"The laudanum must have worn off. It was helping him sleep." She picked up one of the medicine bottles.

"I'm mixing a small dose with brandy. It keeps him comfortable."

"Only it ain healing his wound, Mistress."

"I know." Her voice sounded resigned. Uncorking the medicine bottle, she poured a scant amount into a glass. "But I hate to see him in such pain. And now I'm running out of laudanum."

"Perhaps you could try Mamie's herbs. . . ."

"No," Mistress cut her off. Reaching around Abby, she poured brandy from the decanter into the glass. "I need to go into town. Dr. Preston has the medicine I need, although he charges me dearly. Thank you for watching over him, Abby. You may go."

"Yes Ma'am. If you need me later just holler."

"The laudanum should make him sleep until morning. Perhaps then he'll be feeling stronger. And Abby, don't pay heed to Mister's ramblings. It's just the fever talking."

"I understand," Abby replied, but as soon as she left the room a smile broke over her face. The fever might be making Mister Hammond talk, but now her Mama had a name! *Lively*. A most beautiful name!

A thump followed by the sound of scattering feet came from Miss Julia's room.

Abby frowned. *Cyril*. Something was going to have to be done about that boy. Since freedom, he'd been as wild and troublesome as a rabbit in the garden.

Hands on her hips, she strode into the room, dark except for the gray wash of moonlight coming in through the window. "Cyril! What you doin' in here?"

There was no answer. Abby searched under Miss Julia's bed and in her wardrobe, sure the pesky boy was hiding. But he wasn't in any of his usual places.

Puzzled, Abby scratched her head. If the noise wasn't Cyril . . . then who?

Turning, she spied a book on the floor in front of the bookshelf. Abby had *never* left a precious book on the floor. Had it fallen from the shelf? Is that what had made the thump?

Hurrying over, she picked it up and goosebumps prickled her arms. It was *The History of Little Goody Two-Shoes.*

Miss Julia's favorite book.

✳ ✳ ✳

CHAPTER *Seven*

"'Chapter One. How and About Little Margery and Her Brother,'" Abby read out loud to Mamie and Pap from *The History of Little Goody Two-Shoes*. It was a warm evening, and all three were in the front yard of Hammond House enjoying the last light before the sun set. Since freedom, Abby had boldly read whenever and wherever she could steal a precious instant.

Abby was leaning against the trunk of an ancient oak, the book in her lap. Pap and Mamie were sitting on the steps. Mamie was knitting a sock using yarn unraveled from one of Mister's vests. Pap was mending a broken strap on Toby's harness.

"'Care and discontent shortened the days of Little Margery's father,'" Abby began the story. "'He was forced from his family—'"

"My, my," Mamie said. "Like Rufus forced from Tissie and Cyril."

"No, Mamie, Margery's father died," Abby explained. "Jest listen." She continued reading, "'He was seized with a violent fever in a place where Dr. James's Powder was not to be had, and where he died miserably.'"

"Dr. James's Powder, ha!" Mamie cut in. "Sounds like he need some of my golden seal mixed wid—"

"Mamie, it's a story from long ago. Maybe they didn't have golden seal."

"Poo. I bet dey did." Mamie waved at her. "Now go on wid your story."

"'Margery's poor mother survived the loss of her husband but a few days, and died of a broken heart, leaving Margery and her brother to the wide world.'"

"What she do!" Mamie exclaimed. "Leave her two chillens on account of a broken heart? Why dat the foolest thing I ever heard!"

"Mamie!"

Bending over the harness, Pap's shoulders heaved with laughter.

"It's not funny." Abby shut the book with a snap. "This was Miss Julia's favorite book. Last night, I found it on the floor. I think Miss Julia put it there because it holds a message from my Mama. From *Lively*." She announced the name she'd been holding inside all day, not able to contain it any longer.

Pap quit laughing. Mamie's head jerked back. "Where you git that name?"

Abby scrambled to her feet, the book dropping to the ground. "What's wrong with knowin' her name?"

"Because there no need to hear it." Mamie rose stiffly from the su "Your mama dead to you, Abby. As she dead to me. Knowin' her name woan bring her back."

"Julia said she's not dead!"

"Julia?" Scowling, Mamie stabbed her knitting needles toward Pap. "See what your tales are doin' to dis youngun? Dey makin' her believe in haunts!"

"Miss Julia *did* come." Abby insisted. "Least her spirit did. At first I thought it was jest Mister's feverish ramblins. But Miss Julia visited last night, and she say my mama on earth. That means she not dead to you *or* me!" Abby trembled with anger. "An' that means I'm going to find out about her, Mamie. No matter what you say." Grabbing the book, Abby slipped it into her apron pocket as she fled the front yard. This time, she wasn't just running away. She was running for a reason.

And the reason was *Kennedy*. Maybe no one would talk about Lively. But someone might talk about Kennedy.

And she knew just who that someone might be.

In the quarters, Abby found Uncle Zee and Tissie rocking on his front porch, holding hands. Zee was smoking a corncob pipe, the smoke keeping the gnats and mosquitoes away.

Flopping down on the porch step, Abby stared from one to the other. Tissie's expression was soft and dreamy; Zee's was content.

"Are you two courtin'?" she asked.

"We might be," Uncle Zee replied.

Tissie giggled like a young girl. "We might be gettin' married soon as harvest over."

Abby's jaw dropped.

"Better shut yo' mouth 'fore you swallow a fly," Zee teased.

"Well, I'll be. What does Cyril think 'bout it?"

Tissie raised her eyes to heaven. "Dat boy *need* a father. Runnin' wild all day long. Cain't git him to do a lick of work."

"Maybe he needs a good *whippin'*," Abby suggested.

Zee quit rocking. "Doan want to hear that word in the quarters, Miss Abby," he scolded.

"'Cause of white men like *Kennedy*?" Abby asked.

Tissie glanced hesitantly at Zee. Furrowing his brow, he blew out a cloud of smoke before taking the pipe from his mouth and pointing the stem at Abby. "Yes, because of men like Kennedy. Men who are mean jest for the sake of it."

Abby leaned forward, all eyes and ears. The sun was

low behind the mountains, and she shivered in the cooling air. "Tell me 'bout Kennedy. He whipped my Pa, didn't he? That's why Pa ran away."

For a long while, Zee puffed on his pipe, Tissie rocking silently beside him. Finally, he spoke. "I came to the plantation after Kennedy so I doan know what all happened. I do know he was the overseer before me and the slaves called him the Devil. Mister sent him packin' after he almost kilt a slave."

"My pa, Gabe?" Abby asked. "Did he almost kill my pa?"

Zee shook his head. "All I knowed is that when Master Hammond brought me to the farm, Kennedy and your pa were both gone."

"What about Lively?"

Tissie and Zee gave her surprised looks.

"Mister Hammond told me her name," Abby explained, not wanting to go into the story of Julia's visit.

"Lively was gone, too," Tissie said quietly. "Kennedy, Gabe, Lively—all three were gone. Even deir memories were gone. Master, Mistress, Mamie—no one would say deir names. Acted like none of dem ever lived at Hammond Plantation."

"But they *did*," Abby declared.

"Yes 'um, dey did." Reaching out, Tissie patted Abby's head. "And you proves it. When I came, you was a babe playin' at Mamie's feet. Oh, how your grandma loved you. Still, everyone knew you weren't her babe. And dere were rumors flyin' 'round the quarters—"

"Like what?"

"Like the Devil took your ma and pa," Zee cut in. "Like patrollers chopped them into pieces and buried them in the ground. Ugly rumors that had no truth. That's why I paid them no mind. That's why I worked hard and proved to Master I could be the field boss. That he didn't need no white overseer with a whip to make the hands work."

Abby knew from Zee's firm tone that he was finished talking about Gabe and her Mama. Disappointed, she slowly got to her feet.

Tissie leaned forward in her rocker. "Abby, one thing I knowed for sure: when I first came to Hammond House, it was a sorrowful place. As if Lively had stolen all de laughter when she left. As if keeping all those secrets was sad, hard work for Master, Mistress, and your grandma. You were the only light until Miss Julia was born. Den things grew happy." With a sigh, Tissie began rocking again. "Until de war broke out."

Abby worried her lip as she pondered all the new information. Kennedy, Gabe, and Lively had all vanished about the same time. Why? What had happened? And how would she find out?

Seemed that Tissie and Zee had told her all they knew. Pap claimed to know nothing, and Mister Hammond only spoke with the fever.

That left Mistress, who fainted when Abby mentioned Lively.

Why all the secrets? Abby had no idea, but she felt in her bones that fourteen years ago something powerfully bad must have happened at Hammond House.

✳ ✳ ✳

The drone of bees sent Abby to quivering. She dodged as several darted from the hole in the trunk of the hollow tree. Beside her, Pap was bent over lighting scraps of hemp rope coiled in a tin coffeepot. At his feet were his "honey hunting tools," as he liked to call them.

Abby had draped a scrap of old gauzy curtain over her straw hat and worn a pair of Mistress's gloves to protect her from the bees. But Pap was bare headed and bare handed, claiming a few stings never hurt anybody.

"Those the guard bees 'round the entrance," Pap explained as he blew on the smoldering rope. "Smoke will calm them down. They think it's a forest fire so they fill their stomachs wit honey like they preparin' to flee. Full stomachs make them content—jest like you and me after eatin' Mamie's roast possum."

When a bee zoomed past, Abby danced nervously. Pap had told her not to show fear. "Bees can sense it," he told her. But it was hard when they buzzed so close.

"How'd you git to know so much 'bout bees?" she asked.

"Orchards need bees to be fruitful." He lifted the coffeepot. "There, we got some good smoke. You hold it up close to the hole." He handed it to her. "Trick is gettin' out the honey without ruining the hive. Some honey hunters chop down the whole tree. Me, I want these bees right here making honey all year round."

Gripping the handle of the coffeepot, Abby aimed the funnel of smoke toward the bees, which disappeared inside the tree. Pap thumped on the trunk with the handle of his hatchet. "Doan want to disturb the queen," he explained. "Try to chop right into the combs."

"This sound right." Using a saw, he cut a top and bottom line in the bark and then used the hatchet to make two side cuts. "This be our door. Open it right into the hive." After he'd marked a rectangular piece, he carefully pried it out with a bar.

"Aim some smoke in here," Pap said, pointing to the hole. "It'll chase the bees into another part of the hollow."

Abby held the coffeepot higher. She turned her head, but the smoke stung her eyes and irritated her nose, and she sneezed. When she looked back, Pap's arm was elbow deep in the hole. A minute later, he pulled out a chunk of comb, the broken cells dripping with golden honey.

Abby licked her lips. "Oh, Pap, that looks pure delightful."

"I'll jest take two more pieces. Cain't be greedy." Pap set the comb carefully in the empty bucket. "Or the bees woan invite us back. Now open your mouth and close your eyes."

Abby obeyed, and Pap placed a small piece of comb on her tongue. Slowly, she bit down, honey burst in her mouth, and the sweetness made her swoon.

"Youngun, hold that coffeepot still," Pap warned as he again reached inside the tree, "or those guard bees will teach us a lesson we never forget. One sting won't hurt but a peck of stings like to kill us." When the bucket was full, he picked up the plug of wood and used the end of the hatchet to tap it back into place. "Nice and snug. Now let's skeedaddle before those bees figure they been robbed."

Still carrying the smoking pot, Abby hurried down the hill. Her veil caught on a branch and tore off her hat, and for a second she panicked, afraid the bees were chasing her. But it was only Pap, wheezing as he trundled after her, tools and bucket in hand.

"They ain comin' gal," he assured her.

"Good." Using the lid of the coffeepot for a scoop, Abby sprinkled dirt onto the rope to smother the fire. Then she untangled her veil. As she put her hat on, she looked back at the honey tree, which from a distance looked ordinary. "It's good we made those notches or we'd never find it again."

"And that's the way I aim to keep it." Pap pointed the handle of the hatchet at her. "Doan you tell no one at the quarters 'bout our tree. They'll chop it down, drag it to the farm, and that'll be the end of our honey."

She crossed her heart. "I woan. No one will ever find it. Even this close, you cain't tell it's a honey tree."

Pap chuckled. "Bees too smart to hang out a sign sayin' 'honey' for fear every bear be knockin' on their door."

Abby picked up the bucket and coffeepot. "I guess even bees keep secrets," she said as she led the way home, following the notched trail. Earlier, she'd told Pap about Kennedy, Gabe, and Lively.

"Reckon most critters have secrets. Hard as I've looked, I've never found a hummingbird's nest or a fox den." Pap lowered his voice. "Why even your old grandpa has a secret."

Abby stopped so fast he almost ran into her. "What?"

"If I tell, it woan be a secret." Setting the saw on his shoulder, Pap walked around her.

"You better tell!" She hurried after him, the bucket banging against her knee.

"Nope. 'Cause then you tell Mamie."

"Why would I tell Mamie? She keepin' secrets from me."

"Well, all right." Pap acted all huffy like he hated to give in, but Abby could tell by his grin that he was plum excited to share the news. "Next week, we goin' to Tomasford, and me and Mamie goin' to be married proper by Preacher Simmons."

"Oh, Pap!" Dropping the bucket, Abby gave him a hug. "Mamie'll be so happy."

He put a finger to his lips. "Doan breathe a word."

"Am I comin'?" Abby asked, half afraid to find out the answer.

"Fo' sure."

"Oh, glory days!" Abby twirled beside him. "I never been to town! It'll be so exciting! Shops, sidewalks, goods to buy. And . . .and . . ." Her eyes grew round. "And I can look for Mama!"

"No, Miss Abby, you will not look for your Mama," Pap said sternly. "It's Mamie's special day and nothin' goin' to ruin it."

"Oh, all right," Abby agreed aloud, but inside her mind was afire. Tomasford wasn't big like Charlottesville, but it was the closest town and somewhere, someone had to know about her Mama. Maybe she was working in a shop, or, even better, hunting up and down the streets, looking for Abby.

Abby glanced at Pap, striding down the path ahead of her like an old bandy-legged rooster. When they went to Tomasford, she'd be fox-sly. He'd *never* know she was hunting for her Mama.

Because just like Pap said—*all critters have secrets.*

✳ ✳ ✳

As Mistress explained about sums, Abby nodded dutifully. Since Miss Julia hated arithmetic, Teacher had steered away from numbers, and now the signs and numerals written on the slate made little sense.

She wiggled in the chair seat and Mistress sighed. They were working at the dining room table. During last winter's snowstorm, the school desks in Miss Julia's room had been chopped up for kindling.

"Abby, I can tell that just like Julia your mind is elsewhere. However, one day when you spend your wages in town, you'd better know how to calculate correctly, or the shop owners will only be too glad to cheat you."

Abby pricked her ears at the talk of money. "One day you'll pay me real wages?"

Mistress smiled. "Perhaps after harvest. You've been a huge help the last few days. That honey you and Elisha brought back was a treat. Last night, Mister Hammond devoured an entire hoecake, even licking up the honey that had dripped on the plate. It's the first real food he's eaten in days."

Abby picked at a ragged fingernail, wishing she could convince Mistress that Mamie's doctorin' would set Mister Hammond right. For an educated woman, Mistress could be as mulish as Toby.

"Now. Let's try this again." Mistress erased the slate with a damp rag. Picking up the chalk, she drew a picture of a bonnet. "Let's say you have two and a half dollars, and you wish to buy a bonnet for one dollar and a quarter."

Abby shook her head. "No, Ma'am. I'd never buy a bonnet. My straw hat be fine."

"Abby, we're just pretending."

"Like me and Miss Julia used to pretend we princesses?"

"Yes, like that."

"Then I'll pretend I'm buying a bonnet. Only it's not for me. It's for my Mama, *Lively*."

Mistress gave Abby a startled look. "What did you say?"

"I'm buyin' a bonnet for my Mama, *Lively*," Abby repeated, amazed at the words spilling from her. It had been days since she'd spoken to Mistress about the forbidden subject, but the fear of the root cellar had dimmed and freedom had given her the courage to speak.

"Who told you about Lively?"

"Mister Hammond tol' me."

"No. He *wouldn't* have." Mistress hugged her arms tightly as if she was cold.

"Why not? Why my Mama such a secret?"

"There's no secret," Mistress insisted. "Mister didn't know what he was saying. It—it was just the fever talking."

"Might be the fever, but I believed him," Abby said firmly. "'Sides, what matters is that Lively's my Mama and I deserves to know what happened to her. Least you know that Miss Julia is safe with Jesus."

"Only there's nothing to tell!" Mistress stood abruptly, her arms still folded, her spine rigid.

"I doan believe you. You didn't faint the other day 'cause of nothin'!"

Anger sparked in Mistress's eyes. "Lessons are over for today, Abby." She tossed the chalk on the slate. "And if you continue with you impertinence, your *interrogations*, there will be no more lessons. *Ever*."

Turning sideways in the chair, Abby looked up at her. "But Mistress, why won't you tell me 'bout—"

"Because there is nothing to tell!" Mistress flared. "You've got to quit fooling yourself, Abby. No good can come from searching for your Mama. It's been too long. I won't let you go on some wild goose chase to find her either. *I won't lose you, too!*" she exclaimed, distress coloring her words, and twisting away with a ruffle of skirts, she fled from the dining room.

Abby pressed her palm against her chest, trying to still her nerves. A week ago she never would have challenged Mistress. But hearing her Mama's name had made her bold. Not that she'd gotten any answers about her Mama. At least this time Mistress hadn't fainted. In truth, she'd gotten all riled up.

Abby pondered Mistress's angry words. What had she meant when she said, "I won't lose you too"? Had Lively run away? Had Mistress sent her away? *Or* was Mistress talking about *all* the slaves that had fled Hammond House during the years of the war?

Picking up the chalk, Abby wrote *Livelee. Lively. Livelie.* She wondered which one of those spelled out her Mama's name.

Abby wasn't certain why the mention of Lively upset Mistress. But she tucked Mistress's words in her mind along with *Kennedy* and *Lively* and everything else she'd learned, sure that one day soon she'd puzzle out the answers.

* ❋ *

CHAPTER *Eight*

Abby stuck her finger into the steaming tub of water.
Jest right. Humming, she pulled her soiled dress over her
head. Mamie had hung a quilt over the washroom doorway for privacy, but Abby was still jittery, expecting
pesky Cyril to poke his nappy head around at any
moment.

Hurrying, she dropped her drawers, climbed into
the tub, and slid into the chin-high water. She couldn't
remember the last time she'd had a bath.

The quilt rippled like a curtain in a breeze. "Cyril!
You better not come in here," she warned. "'Less you
want me to dunk you in this tub."

Pushing aside the quilt, Mamie bustled into the
room carrying clothes and a towel. "Chile, soap yourself

from head to toe," she ordered. "Though why we be makin' such a fuss 'bout goin' to town, I doan know."

Mamie still doesn't know Pap's secret! Smiling to herself, Abby stuck her nose under the water and blew a mess of bubbles. Since morning, the household had been preparing for tomorrow's trip, and for once joy filled Hammond House.

Picking up the chunk of soap, Abby ran it over her hair. "What you got there, Mamie?" she asked, her gaze on the clothes draped over her grandma's arm.

Mamie's eyes twinkled. "You talkin' 'bout dese old rags?" She held up a blue and white checked dress, its scooped neck bordered with white lace. Under the dress was a chemise of fine cotton. "Dress used to be Missus's. A little tuck here, a little hemming dere, and it fit you perfectly."

Abby grinned. She'd never worn such finery! "Thank you, Mamie."

"Thank Missus." Mamie rubbed Abby's sudsy head. "Now scurry before your water git cold."

Later, Abby was brushing her hair in front of the kitchen fire. Wearing her new checked dress, her hair sweet and soft, she felt like a fine lady.

A commotion of voices came from Mamie and Pap's room. When she peeked in, she saw Tissie lacing Mamie into the bodice of a green velvet dress. Her grandma's head wrap was off and her gray hair had been coiled in a bun. On the bed was a saucy peaked hat with a green plume.

"Mamie!" Abby exclaimed. "Is that you?"

Mamie grunted. "It's me all right. Missus say I cain wear dis dress tomorrow, though if Tissie keep tightening the bodice, the seams may bust first."

Abby giggled as she crossed to the bed. "Next you'll be wearing frilled petticoats and a hoop."

"Lordy no." Mamie laughed along with her. "Not in that bumpety old wagon."

Picking up the hat, Abby ran her fingers along the feather, remembering the last time she'd seen the velvet dress. It was years ago, when the war first began and the South had seceded from the Union. She'd hidden in the bushes and watched Master Hammond, proud in his new Confederate uniform, escort Mistress to the waiting carriage and its team of high-prancing horses. Mistress had worn the velvet outfit, her waist tiny, the bell-shaped skirt and hat plume swaying gracefully with each step. Jake, the coachman, had driven them to a party at a neighboring plantation where Mistress and Master had toasted a quick victory for the South.

Now there was no coachman, no carriage, no high-prancing horses, parties, or victory. But tomorrow, for the first time in her life, Abby was going to town in her new dress to look for her Mama—and that was excitement enough!

✳ ✳ ✳

Early morning, when Abby walked onto the front porch, Pap was waiting beside Toby and the wagon. He wore Mister's old black bowler and topcoat. Abby skipped down the walkway carrying her straw hat. "You look fine, Pap, but Toby as ugly as ever."

Pap hooked his thumbs in the lapels of his coat. "Toby doan need to look handsome. He ain gettin' married today." He nodded at her. "You look fine yourself, Miss Abby."

Abby blushed. "Why thankee. kind sir." She plucked a dried apple from her skirt pocket and fed it to Toby. "Do you think he'll get us all the way to Tomasford?" she asked, patting his neck.

"Oh, he'll get us there. It jest will be a powerful slow trip."

"That's fine with me. I want to see all the sights!"

"Pap? What you wearin'?" Mamie came onto the porch, Mistress beside her. Mamie wore the velvet dress and plumed hat. Mistress wore a somber gray silk dress with a high neck. Her hair was parted in the center, smoothed back in a no-nonsense coil, and covered with a black net. She carried a drawstring purse and parasol.

"I might ask you the same, Mamie," Pap said as he

hurried toward them. "You look as lovely as a peacock. Now allow me to escort you fine ladies to your waitin' carriage and team of fiery stallions."

Mamie guffawed, and Mistress hid a smile behind her gloved hand.

"Abby, there are some empty feed sacks in the wagon bed so you'll be more comfortable," Mistress said as the three came down the walk.

Pap helped Mamie then Mistress onto the wagon seat. Using the spokes of the wheel like a ladder, Abby climbed into the wagon bed, which was already loaded with several baskets. Her skirt caught on the carriage seat and she fell in a heap on the lumpy sacks, which let out a yelp.

Startled, Abby scrambled to a sitting position. She lifted a corner of a sack. Cyril's big eyes stared at her from underneath. He put a finger to his lips. Abby frowned and shook her head no. She didn't want Cyril coming to town. He'd mess up all her plans.

"Please doan tell," he pleaded.

Abby rolled her eyes and dropped the edge of the sack. Then she spread out her skirt and made herself comfortable, purposefully leaning her weight against him. Tissie was staying home to nurse Mister Hammond, who was still bed bound. She was used to Cyril running off, but by dark she'd be worried sick.

When they got home late tonight, Cyril would get a whipping for sure.

When everyone was seated Pap flapped the reins on Toby's back, and the wagon rolled forward. Abby clutched the side as they lurched down the lane. The sun was rising behind Hammond House, and morning mist covered the yard like a quilt.

Looks like a picture in one of Miss Julia's books, Abby thought as the house receded farther into the distance with each rise and fall of Toby's hooves. When the wagon rounded the bend, Abby spotted three men working in the fallow cornfield. She recognized Uncle Zee's slouch hat, Buck's wide shoulders, and Mitchell's skinny arms. Zee and Buck were hitched up to the plow while Mitchell walked behind guiding it. Abby imagined the sweat rolling from their brows, their muscles straining with each stride.

She raised her hand to wave, but then quickly lowered it, afraid to invite their envy. They were working like mules while she was bound for town behind one.

Soon Mister's fields gave way to unfamiliar countryside, and Abby's insides hummed like buzzing flies. What would Tomasford be like? Would patrollers stop them before they got to town? What if they got lost? *What if Mama isn't there!*

Cyril stirred beneath her backside. "Git off me, you brick," he whispered hoarsely.

Abby shifted sideways and his head popped from beneath a sack. "We dere yet?" he asked, failing to keep his voice low.

"We barely off Mister's land," Abby whispered. "Woan be there 'til after noon."

"After noon! When we eat? My stomach as hollow as . . ." his brow puckered ". . . as *your* head." He giggled at his joke.

Abby kicked him. "Should have thought of that before you decided to stow away."

Without turning in the carriage seat, Mamie said, "No one go hungry in dis wagon. I packed 'nough for four people *and* one skinny boy."

Grinning, Cyril threw back the sack and scrambled to a sitting position. "Thank you, Mamie!"

Pap glanced over his shoulder. "Cyril, what you doin' here, boy?"

"I jest had to come on dis big adventure," he announced happily.

Abby wrinkled her nose. "Least you could have washed. Smell like a fish."

"Your mother will be frantic, Cyril." Mistress turned sideways in the seat to look at him, then said to Pap, "Elisha, perhaps we should turn back."

Cyril bolted to his knees. "No, Ma'am. Please doan turn back. I tole Lanny to tell my mama where I be after I gits a head start. If I go back now, Mama thrash me for sure."

Mamie snorted. "An you deserves every lash."

Mistress tapped her cheek as if considering it. "Well, all right. If we turn around, it would add another two hours to the journey. We'd probably have to postpone our trip."

"Oh, thank you Missus!" Cyril hopped on his knees. "I jest had to be at the church when Pap and Mamie git married!"

Abby kicked Cyril for letting out the secret but it was too late. She held her breath, expecting to hear a bellow from Mamie, but the only sound was the crunch of the wheels on the road. When Abby turned to look, she saw Mamie's head resting on Pap's shoulder and heard snuffling. Was her grandma crying?

Then Pap put his arm around Mamie's waist, the hat plume quivered, and Abby knew that if her grandma *was* crying it was from pure happiness.

As the wagon continued slowly east, the sun rose in the sky. Abby put on her straw hat and Mistress opened her parasol. Cyril dozed, his head in Abby's lap. Abby tried to stay awake. She didn't want to miss a thing even though the only sights seemed to be trees, birds, scrubby fields, dusty road, and more trees. Now she knew why no one came calling at Hammond House.

Finally, when the sun was overhead and Abby's bottom was sore from the bumpy ride, Mistress said, "Pull off here, Elisha."

Abby straightened. *Are we coming into Tomasford?* But all she saw was a ramshackle cabin set off the road in a small clearing.

Abby tapped Cyril on the head. "Git up lazy bones."

"Are we goin' to eat?" he asked sleepily.

"Whoa, mule." Pap halted Toby. Jumping off the wagon seat, he hurried to the other side to help Mistress down. "Abby, will you please hand me that picnic basket?" she asked as she closed her parasol and set it on the seat.

"Yes, Ma'am." Abby passed the larger basket from the wagon. Curious, she scooted next to Cyril to see what was going on. A woman appeared on the porch of the cabin with a little girl propped on one hip. A boy about Abby's age came out to stand beside her. He was holding the hand of a second girl. All four were as scrubby and skinny as cornhusk scarecrows.

And they were white.

Abby blinked in astonishment.

"Hello, Mrs. Tucker," Mistress said in greeting as she walked down the dirt path to the house. "I brought you some supplies."

A small garden was planted on one side of the path, but the dirt looked parched and poor. The rest of the yard was hard packed earth and weeds. Abby scanned the cleared area around the cabin. She saw no hog pens or hogs, chicken coops or chickens. There was no firewood stacked against the wall, no smoke curling from the chimney.

"Pap," Abby whispered. "Who's that?"

"The Tuckers. All their menfolk die in the war."

"What do they eat?"

Pap shook his head. "I doan know, chile. I doan know."

Abby watched as Mistress handed the woman the basket and they went inside the cabin. The tall boy hopped off the porch. Thumbs hooked in the waistband of his britches, he sauntered down the path. Abby stared at him. She'd never seen a white boy her age. His cheeks and belly were sunken with hunger and his hair was as wild as a hayfield, but when he strode toward them, he tipped his chin high.

"That's Dewey Tucker, the only boy left," Pap said in a low voice. "He tryin' to do a man's job."

When Mistress came back onto the porch carrying the basket, she was alone. Dewey barely nodded to her as she went past. Thumbs still hooked, he rocked back on his bare heels and watched silently as she boarded the wagon, and they drove off.

"He didn't even thank you," Abby said when they were out of earshot.

"Mrs. Tucker thanked me," Mistress said. "Dewey's too proud. He's just like his father and big brother, God rest their souls." She sighed. "Little Ellie and Jane pounced on the cornbread and honey like starving puppies. I only wish I could have brought them more."

"When *we* gonna eat?" Cyril asked.

Abby scowled at him. "Is your own belly all you can think about?"

"Why, yes 'um it is. 'Specially when it makin' so much racket."

"We'll pull off 'bout a mile up yonder," Pap said. "There's a shady place to stop before we git to the main road. Toby need to fill his belly, too, Cyril."

They picnicked under a beech tree by a stream. Pap took the bit from Toby's mouth and hooked a nosebag filled with corn to his headstall. After eating dried peaches and cold rabbit pie, Mamie and Pap stretched out on the quilt for a short nap. Mistress put on her bonnet and walked toward a shady grove, a book in one hand. Abby dangled her feet in the cool stream water while Cyril hopped along the bank trying to catch a frog in the weeds.

Hoof beats on the hard road made Abby scramble to her feet. Five riders on horses were trotting toward them, a cloud of dust masking their faces. Abby's mouth went dry. Pap jumped up and pulled Mamie to her feet. And although he carefully adjusted the bowler hat on his head, panic sharpened his features.

Grabbing Cyril by the shirt, Abby swung him behind her. "Git down in the cattails. *Stay out of sight,*" she hissed, and for once he obeyed.

The riders halted their horses. The men wore cobbled together uniforms—Union mixed with Confederate— as if they'd stolen their outfits from any fallen soldier. One man had no eye. One had no arm. Their horses' sides heaved from hard riding.

Abby tried to swallow, but fear and dust clogged her throat as she put a name to the men in front of her. *Patrollers.* Men who, until this instant, had existed only in the stories told around the fire at the quarters—and in her nightmares.

❋ ❋ ❋

CHAPTER *Nine*

"May I see your passes?" the lead man asked. He sported a scruffy beard, military vest, and gray cap. "Your proof of employment?"

Taking off his bowler, Pap stepped forward. "We have no passes, sir," he replied politely. "No proof of employment."

The man cocked one bushy brow. "Did you hear that, boys?" he called over his shoulder to the other riders. "I believe these coloreds think they're free to roam the countryside like gypsies."

The four men started chuckling, and chills rose up Abby's arms. She searched frantically for Mistress. *Where is she!*

"How about we show them what free really means?"

the man continued as he uncoiled a whip hanging from his pommel.

"Sir, we ain gypsies," Pap said hastily. "We on our way to Tomasford from Hammond Plantation."

The man spat a stream of tobacco at Pap's feet. "That's not what it looks like to me." He jutted his thumb toward the wagon. "Looks to me like you three coloreds are running off with a stolen wagon and mule. Thieves, I'll wager, and we aim to serve justice. Right, boys?"

"You have no right callin' us thieves," Mamie spoke up, but Pap hushed her with a flap of his hand. "Sir, my family has done nothing wrong." He addressed the leader, his chin tipped proudly. "Take justice out on me."

"Fine with me, old uncle." The man with the beard dismounted and handed his horse's reins to the rider beside him.

"Elisha, no." Mamie plucked at Pap's coat sleeve, but he patted her arm and said, "It'll be all right." After putting on his hat, he knelt in the road, his frail, hunched back toward the whip.

For a second Abby stood frozen with fear, but when the man snaked back his arm, she raced to Pap. "No! Doan whip my grandpa!" she hollered, covering his back with her body. "Whip me!"

"Abby, this not your fight!" Pap twisted around trying to toss her off, but she clung to him like a burr. For a second the bearded man paused, then he chuckled. "Fine with me. One black back the same as the next."

Oh please, Dear Lord forget my sins and make this whipping mercifully short. Abby scrunched her eyes tightly, waiting for the sting of the lash. Instead someone grabbed her arm and drew her upright.

"What is the meaning of this!" Mistress exclaimed, her fury directed at the men as she pulled first Abby then Pap to their feet. "What in the name of Heaven do you men think you are doing?"

The bearded man lowered his whip. "Ma'am. My name is Corporal Perry Smythe." He tipped his cap. "And this is my band of men. We're stopping, interviewing, and punishing all vagrants and thieves."

"I don't care if you're General Robert E. Lee!" Mistress said, her voice rising. "These good folks are not runaways or thieves. They are free men and ladies. They need no passes to travel these roads!"

"Begging your pardon, Ma'am. We aim to see that no coloreds travel without proof of employment. And all vagrants will be arrested."

"And who has given you this power?"

"Why, we appointed ourselves," Smythe replied importantly. "You won't believe the number of coloreds we've had to whip."

Abby inhaled sharply at the horrible image. Had they

caught Rafe and Sally? What about Malinda, Joseph, and Able? And what about her Mama thirteen years ago? Had any of them made it to freedom? Abby wrung her hands, realizing now that Mistress hadn't been lying to the field hands when she'd told them of the patrollers' lawlessness.

"Corporal Smythe. These folks are in my employ," Mistress explained, her voice quivering. "This is my wagon and mule. They have stolen nothing. Now let us pass without further harassment."

Smythe grinned, showing rotten teeth. "I would, Ma'am, except how do me and the boys know *you're* telling the truth?" Leaning close to Mistress, he poked at her with a tobacco-stained finger. "You might be dressed fine, but how do we know *you* ain't a slave-loving thief?"

Mistress's hand shot out and slapped him soundly on the cheek. "How dare you!"

Astonished by the blow, Smythe staggered.

"How dare you speak to me with such insolence," Mistress repeated, her eyes crackling like embers. "My name is Mrs. Rebecca Hammond. I am the wife of Captain John Hammond of the Fifth Virginia Infantry of the Stonewall Brigade. If he were here, he'd have you court-martialed for your shameful behavior."

Corporal Smythe whisked off his cap. "Excuse me,

Ma'am. I didn't realize you were Captain Hammond's wife." He glanced at the mule and wagon as if puzzled by their poor means of transportation. "I'm sorry we bothered you and your slaves."

"*Workers,*" Mistress corrected haughtily.

"Give my regards to Captain Hammond." Bowing slightly, he put on his cap. "And have a pleasant journey."

Coiling up his whip, Smythe mounted. Abby watched the men wheel their horses and trot off. When they disappeared, she began to tremble.

"It's all right now, Abby," Mistress said, her own words fraught with emotion. "They're gone."

"Thank you, Missus, for coming to our aid," Pap said softly.

Just then Cyril burst from the weeds, brandishing a knobby stick. "Come back you ruffians," he hollered to the empty road, "so I can whap you good!"

Everyone laughed with relief.

"They would have shot you dead, youngun," Pap said, ruffling the boy's hair.

Turning, Mistress faced the group. Her bonnet was crooked. Dust smudged her cheeks. "Mamie, Elisha, I— I'm so sorry."

"No, Ma'am. There nothing for you to be sorry 'bout," Pap said as he brushed off the knees of his pants.

"I need to apologize for the behavior of those *renegades.*"

Her nostrils flared with righteous anger. "What has this country come to when free people can't travel the roads without being accosted? When a lone woman must invoke the name of her husband to be believed?" She shook her head. "Incidents like this make me ashamed to call myself a Southerner."

There was an awkward silence. Bending, Abby picked up Pap's bowler from the ground and dusted it off with her skirt. When she handed it to him he winked, but Abby could tell by the pallor of his skin that he was still shaken.

Pap donned his hat, setting it at a rakish angle. Then he crooked his elbows and held them out to Mamie and Mistress. "Come, fine ladies," he said. "Let me escort you to your chariot. We have to hurry if we goin' to make the church on time."

❋ ❋ ❋

The town looks smaller and dustier than I imagined, Abby thought as the wagon rumbled down the street into Tomasford. Earlier, as they'd traveled south on the main road, they'd passed torn-up fencing, abandoned shacks, barren fields, and rundown barns—all remnants of the hardships caused by the long war. The town itself consisted of a handful of squat buildings connected with wooden walkways designed to keep boots and skirts from the mud.

Abby wasn't sure if her disappointment with the town was because the trip had been tainted by their meeting with the renegades or because she'd expected Tomasford to be as grand as the city of New York. No matter which, she realized; if her Mama had safely run away, she probably wouldn't be living in such a bare-bones place.

Frowning to herself, Abby realized another problem: She had no idea what Lively looked like. And Lively had no idea of her! How would they know each other? And why hadn't she thought of this before?

She bit at a ragged fingernail, deciding that the answer was to stick close to Mamie or Mistress who, though mulish when it came to speaking about Lively, would surely recognize the woman they'd both known thirteen years ago.

As the wagon rattled slowly through town, Abby read the shop signs aloud. "Tate's General Store, Tomasford Inn, Peterson's Granary." They passed a farrier hammering a horseshoe, a wheelwright mending a spoke, a shopkeeper sweeping his stoop: All signs that life had returned to Tomasford since the war was over.

Propped on his knees, Cyril clung to the side of the wagon and stared with open-mouthed wonder at the sights. In contrast, Abby's gaze flitted from the road to the walks to the doorways as she searched for a dark-skinned woman who might be her Mama.

Finally, Pap halted Toby in front of a whitewashed stucco church.

"Captain Hammond and I were married in this church," Mistress said, directing her words to no one in particular. "The day before the wedding, my family and I traveled by carriage from Staunton, which is not a large city compared to Baltimore. However, you can imagine my chagrin at the little town of Tomasford. I loved John, but I began to wonder what I'd gotten into."

Abruptly, she turned toward Mamie. "Oh, what melancholy ramblings," she declared. "Mamie, Elisha, this is your day of celebration, and I must keep my thoughts to myself. Come, let's find Preacher Simmons."

Preacher Simmons hurried from the church before they reached the entrance. "Good afternoon, Rebecca," he greeted Mistress warmly, his fleshy cheeks wobbling as he trotted down the steps. "It's been weeks since you've been to town. How's Mister Hammond?"

"Mister Hammond is not feeling his usual robust self," Mistress replied.

Preacher clucked sympathetically. Abby had stopped a polite distance away with Mamie, Pap, and Cyril, and she noticed Preacher didn't glance once at them.

"I'm so sorry about your husband," Preacher told Mistress. "It pains me to know that one of Nelson

County's most gallant soldiers is in distress." Taking her slim gloved hands in his chubby ones, Preacher led Mistress up the church steps. "What can I do to help?"

"Your prayers are always appreciated," Mistress said. "However, the reason I'm here today—"

"Preacher Simmons is as plump as a piglet," Cyril whispered to Abby, echoing her thoughts as Mistress disappeared with him into the church.

"Must be the Lord looked out for him during the lean times of the war," she whispered back. Abby looked over at Pap, who had moved into the shade of an oak tree. He'd taken off his bowler and was turning it nervously in his hands. Next to him, Mamie stood straight as a fence post, and she, too, wore an anxious expression.

"You two as skittish as calves," Abby said as she walked toward them. "You ain rethinking marriage, are you?"

Pap shook his head. "No, Miss Abby. This frettin' has nothing to do with my marryin' Mamie in a church. That wish be in my heart since I first met your grandma. This has to do with the church not wanting to marry us." He nodded toward the doorway. "Preacher Simmons might not be favorable to folks like us."

"Folks like us?" Abby furrowed her brow.

"Freed slaves," Pap explained.

"But the war's over. President Lincoln made us all equal."

Pap snorted. "Appears the President forgot to tell the men of Nelson County."

"Preacher Simmons is not like those renegades," Abby pointed out. "He's a servant of God. Surely he wants the Lord to bless your union."

Mamie humphed. "As long as God in Heaven and Preacher here on Earth, we be servants to *Preacher's* will."

"Mamie! Elisha!" Mistress called as she swept down the steps, Preacher Simmons following behind her, a Bible in his hands. "Preacher Simmons has *kindly* offered to marry you!" she told them excitedly. "Here outside, under God's blue sky." She waved her arm to indicate the churchyard, a pink flush coloring her cheeks.

Mamie's expression turned stony. Abby's jaw tightened. Pap was right. It didn't matter if they were dressed in Sunday finery. It didn't matter that President Lincoln had set them free. Preacher Simmons didn't want *coloreds* in his church any more than he wanted slaves.

"I doan believe *kindly offered* were his *true* words," Mamie said under her breath.

Taking Mamie's hands in her gloved ones, Mistress smiled imploringly. "Mamie, please. We can make this a joyous occasion."

Pap slid an arm around Mamie's stiff shoulders.

Clearing his throat, he addressed Preacher Simmons. "Thankee suh for your kind offer. It is Mamie's and my dearest wish to be joined legally, in the eyes of God, with the blessings of the church."

"Good, good." Preacher Simmons bobbed his head as he flipped open the Bible. "Then let's get on with the ceremony. Dear Lord, we stand before thee—" he began, his words rushing forth like water. Nevertheless tears rolled down Abby's cheeks when Pap and Mamie faced each other, love in their eyes, and Preacher pronounced them "Man and Wife," before slamming shut the Bible and scurrying into the church without a backward glance.

After the wedding Pap and Mamie took Mistress's tea set and headed to the woodworker's to inquire about a new bed. Cyril stayed behind at the church to graze Toby on the lawn, the promise of gumdrops and taffy hushing his protests. Picking up an empty basket from the wagon bed, Abby followed Mistress toward the shops. She sat on the steps of the inn, which housed the post office, while Mistress went inside to check for mail. Pulling the brim of her straw hat low, she watched for her Mama. At the same time, she tried not to arouse attention. Still, when people passed by they gave her a suspicious stare and a wide berth. One older boy spat at her feet.

Finally Mistress bustled through the inn doors.

"Come, Abby, let's go to Tate's before the hour gets late. Not only do we need provisions, but I hope to buy your grandparents a wedding present."

As they hurried down the street Abby lifted her skirt with one hand, trying to imitate Mistress's ladylike walk despite the mud, manure, and pushy passersby. Minutes later, she followed Mistress into Tate's General Store. "Morning, Mr. Tate," Mistress greeted.

The shopkeeper strode from behind the counter. "Why, Mrs. Hammond! What a pleasure!" he exclaimed, his eyes lighting on the basket on her arm and the drawstring purse dangling from her wrist. "What *can* I do for you this fine day?"

Opening her purse, Mistress drew out a written list, and the two made their way to the counter. For a moment, Abby didn't move, overwhelmed by the goods stacked on shelves and spilling from barrels. Even though some of the shelves and bins were bare, it appeared to her that Tate's stocked almost everything in the world.

Bolts of colorful cloth caught her attention, and she walked over to a table of fabric. Breathless, she fingered a sky blue calico with yellow and blue flowers and picked up a card of eyelet lace. *What beautiful colors. What fancy handiwork. If Mamie would teach me to sew, I could make such a fine dress!*

Behind the counter, Mr. Tate cleared his throat. He

was scowling at Abby under bushy brows. Abby whipped her arms to her sides then glanced anxiously at Mistress, who was browsing among the tables and boxes. She'd never been in a store before. Had she done something wrong?

"Miss, I take it you didn't read the signs on the front door?" Mr. Tate asked.

Of course Abby had read the signs. *No credit alowed. No Confederate Scrip.*

"No suh. I cain't read."

He pursed his lips. "I thought so."

"Though I believe you spelled 'allowed' incorrectly," she added.

The shopkeeper's brows shot to his receding hairline. Mistress stifled a smile. "Why—why, the impertinence!" he sputtered. Raising his arm, he pointed to the door. "I would like you to leave!"

"Why, Mr. Edward Tate," Mistress exclaimed. "I'm surprised at your lack of hospitality."

Mr. Tate's arm shook. "The sign clearly states 'No credit allowed.'"

"But that's not true, Mr. Tate." Mistress whisked around a barrel. "Folks purchase goods from your store on credit every day."

"Not if they're—they're—"

"Colored?" Opening her drawstring purse, Mistress

plucked out three silver coins and handed them to Abby. "Your wages, dear."

Abby gasped. She hadn't seen real United States coins since the war started.

"Where'd you git these?" she whispered as she closed her palms tightly around them.

Mistress smiled mysteriously. "I saved them for a special occasion. And I believe your first trip to town is that special occasion."

Mr. Tate darted around the counter, a greedy look in his eyes. "Real US currency. Well, that changes things. Look around, little girl. Tate's has everything you need."

"At dear prices!" Mistress's expression turned serious. "Ten dollars a pound for sugar? Surely, Mr. Tate, that must be a misprint."

"I can assure you it is not, Mrs. Hammond," Mr. Tate replied smoothly. "The war may be over, but supplies continue to be scarce as hens' teeth. You wouldn't believe how hard I have to scrounge and scramble to stock my shelves." Pulling a handkerchief from his shirt pocket, he mopped his forehead as if exhausted. "However, since you are a valuable customer, I believe we can adjust that price a tiny bit."

Leaving Mistress to her bartering, Abby wandered down the aisle. A new dress would be fine, but what she really wanted was writing paper or a book. She'd read

The History of Little Goody Two-Shoes so many times it was dogeared. And of course, she'd love to buy a wedding present for Mamie and Pap, too. Carefully, she studied every item, noting that the prices *were* dear, and her dollars wouldn't go far.

And don't forget to ask someone about Mama, Abby reminded herself, glancing at Mr. Tate. The shopkeeper would know everyone in Tomasford. If she inquired politely, he might reply. But she'd have to wait until Mistress was occupied elsewhere. She didn't dare bring up Lively's name in front of her again.

As Abby rounded a display of thread, she spotted several newspapers laid out like a fan on the wooden countertop. Picking up the *Charlottesville Express,* she skimmed the pages and columns of tiny black print. A line caught her attention: "Information wanted of one slave woman, Mary Young, about thirty years old, who belonged to Master Charles Buckingham."

Abby gripped the paper as she continued to read, "Mary Young was sold at Auction to a Mister Jackson perhaps going to the Tidewater area of Virginia. Any information concerning her whereabouts thankfully received by her husband, Caleb Young."

Her gaze flew down the page. There was an entire column of advertisements written by freed slaves who were trying to locate loved ones. *That's how I can find*

Mama! Abby thought, hope flaring in her chest. *I'll put an advertisement in the paper!*

Fired up, she composed the words in her head: Information wanted of one Lively Joyner, who once belonged to Master John Hammond of Nelson County. Any information concerning her whereabouts will be thankfully received by her daughter, Miss Abby Joyner, of Hammond Plantation, *who dearly wishes to be reunited with her long lost mother!*

❄ ❄ ❄

CHAPTER *Ten*

"Excuse me, *Miss*, if you're going to read that paper, you must purchase it."

Startled, Abby crinkled the newspaper shut. Mr. Tate was leaning across the counter, not trying to hide the suspicion in his face.

"I would like to buy it, please, suh," Abby said hastily. "But first I have other purchases to make."

Mr. Tate glanced uneasily at the door. "Fine, but be quick about it. I don't want to keep my regular customers waiting."

Since there were no other customers in the store, Abby got his drift. *He wants me to leave.* Carefully, she refolded the newspaper and set it on the counter.

Mistress walked over, plumping a feather pillow.

"What do you think, Abby?" she asked. Abby's mind was still on the paper. How would she place her own advertisement? Who could she get to help her?

"Do you think Elisha and Mamie would like pillows for their new bed?" Mistress went on. "They're rather expensive, but since we no longer have any geese or ducks at Hammond Plantation, we can't make them one."

Drawing her thoughts away from Lively, Abby willed herself to reply, "I think it's a fine weddin' gift. How 'bout I buy material to make pillow slips? And doan forget Cyril's sweets. He'll be fit to be tied if we come back empty handed."

"Thank you for reminding me. Why don't you pick some out for him?" Mistress stuffed two pillows in the larger basket and handed it to Abby. "Here, you can use this for your purchases." Then she glanced down at the smaller basket on her arm. "My, it's about full. I've already traded John's gold pocket watch, and we still need staples." Raising her wrist, she asked Abby to unclasp a charm bracelet that had been hidden under her sleeve. "Fortunately, Mr. Tate's wife has an eye for fine jewelry. *My* fine jewelry in particular," she added in a low voice before heading over to the counter.

As Abby selected candy for Cyril, she thought about the Tuckers. After calculating the cost of the newspaper and the muslin for the pillow slips, she decided she had enough pennies left to buy a bag of sweets for little Ellie and Jane. She wished she had enough for Dewey, but she doubted he'd accept a present from a colored girl.

After Mr. Tate rang up all the purchases and packed them in the baskets, he bid them a hasty farewell. Abby purposefully had not bought the newspaper. Before leaving, she paused at the front door. "Mistress, I forgot one thing. I'll catch up to you outside."

"Let's meet back at the church, Abby," Mistress said. "I need to stop at Dr. Preston's for medicine."

When Abby hurried back to the counter, Mr. Tate gave her an exasperated look.

"Sir, I'd like to buy the *Charlottesville Express*," she said as she set her basket on the counter. Before picking up the paper, she glanced at the front door, glimpsing Mistress's gray silk through the glass pane. Was she looking in? Would she see what Abby was buying?

"Miss, I don't have all day." Mr. Tate drummed his fingers impatiently.

Quickly, Abby paid the fifteen cents and then opened the paper to the information page. "Mr. Tate, sir, can you tell me how I would place an advertisement in this paper?"

Putting on his glasses, Mr. Tate read where she was pointing. "You'd have to go to the office in Charlottesville."

"I cain't do that. It's too far away."

"Or you can send them a telegraph or letter."

"I cain do that!"

"Along with two dollars."

"Two dollars!"

"The advertisements run for a month."

Abby's shoulders fell. She'd just spent all her money on goods. Folding the paper, she hid it in the basket under the pillows.

The door opened with a jingle, and Mr. Tate shoved the basket into her hands. "Just take your things and *leave*," he hissed as he hustled her toward the door, exclaiming, "Why, Mrs. Weaver, you look positively radiant today! You'll be happy to know that I have fresh eggs."

The door slammed shut behind Abby, but she was too upset to notice. Suddenly, the possibility of finding her Mama seemed as hopeless as the mountains of dirty clothes on wash day. Today's money had been a gift. She doubted she'd ever have two dollars again.

Then a thought hit her. *Maybe one of the advertisements in the paper is from my Mama! I can find her that way!*

Buoyed by the new hope, Abby trotted down the sidewalk. She almost ran into Mistress, who was leaving Dr. Preston's office with an anxious expression on her face.

"Bad news?" Abby asked.

Mistress sighed. "Nothing I didn't expect."

When the two reached the churchyard, they found Cyril under the oak tree playing marbles with several town children. Toby was grazing in the churchyard; piles of his manure dotted the grass.

Abby giggled. "One of God's creatures has left his callin' card."

Mistress laughed. "Preacher Simmons will be delighted with the free fertilizer." She plucked the bag of candy from Abby's basket. "Please give this to Cyril. I'll put both baskets in the wagon bed and then bid Preacher good day."

As soon as Cyril saw Abby, he came running. "Where my sweets?" he demanded, his eyes darting warily toward the other children.

"Why you so skittery? 'Fraid the others will want to share your candy?" Abby asked as she held out the bag.

The town children were already scattering for home. Cyril snatched the bag, ran to the church steps, and squatted to inspect the contents. At the same time, Pap and Mamie came down the street, Mamie leaning heavily on his arm.

Abby went to meet them. "How did the bed buyin' go?"

Pap grinned. "Mr. Franklin will craft us a fine bed. Should be ready the end of the month."

"Den we sleep like a king and queen," Mamie said in a faint voice.

"Mamie? Are you all right?"

"Jest worn out from happiness."

Pap led Mamie to the steps. "You sit while me and Abby hitch Toby."

Abby patted her grandma's arm. "Since Toby's belly full of the Lord's grass, he's bound to sprout angel wings and fly us home."

Home. It was the first time Abby had called Hammond House her home. She thought about the Tuckers, the patrollers, Mr. Tate, and the other townsfolk. Had the trip changed her mind about running away to freedom?

Perhaps. But it hadn't changed her mind about finding her Mama. Tonight when she got home she'd read every advertisement in the newspaper until she found one written by her Mama just for her:

Information wanted about one Abby Joyner, female child last held in her mama's arms thirteen years ago. Please contact Lively Joyner, freed woman, who dearly wishes to be reunited with her long lost daughter.

❊ ❊ ❊

It was dark and a light rain was falling when the wagon rumbled down the lane toward Hammond House. "Thank God we're here," Mistress said, echoing everyone's thoughts.

In the wagon bed beside Abby, Cyril slept soundly, covered by sacks, his lips sticky with taffy and gumdrops. On the wagon seat, Mamie sagged against Pap, her eyes shut. After stopping at the Tuckers, even Abby had dozed, the adventure to town having worn her out.

When the wagon halted, Tissie came running down the sidewalk. "Thank the Lord you're here!" she cried. "Mister so feverish he's threatenin' to shoot all the Yankees. Zee hid the guns and knives and we barricaded the door, but oh! We doan know how to calm him."

Closing her parasol, Mistress clambered from the wagon before Pap could assist her. "Thank you, Tissie, for all you've done. I'll handle it from—" Her words trailed off as she fled up the sidewalk toward the house. Cyril stirred. When he saw Tissie, his eyes grew huge.

She shook her finger at him. "Cyril, I have a mind to whip you good. Only I'm too tired to raise my arm— and too happy to see you!" Reaching over the side of the wagon, she gave him a big hug before lifting him out.

"Abby, you take your grandma inside," Pap said. "One of the hands can help me with Toby and the supplies. Doan let her fuss with food or the fire. Git her right in bed."

With one arm around Mamie's waist, Abby guided her up the walkway. Her grandma's velvet dress was damp from the rain, and as they walked she slumped against Abby's side, her breathing and steps labored.

"Mamie, are you all right?"

"I'll be . . . fine . . . chile," she replied, her words coming in gasps. "Jest . . . need . . . to rest."

Slowly, they made their way through the dark house, into the summer kitchen, and into Mamie and Pap's room. Abby helped her grandma to bed. With a low groan, Mamie sank upon the mattress. Quickly, Abby unfastened the buttons and hooks. "Let me git you out of this wet dress. You been strapped tight all day. I bet loosenin' this bodice will make you feel better."

Mamie tried to smile but her teeth were chattering. Finally, Abby got her undressed and under the quilt. Mamie's face was ashen and she pressed her palm against her chest as if in pain. Racing back into the Big House, Abby leaped up the slave stairway. As she ran down the hall, she heard Mistress crooning to Mister. "Just drink this, John. Please. It will chase those nightmares away. Then you will sleep."

Abby dashed into Miss Julia's room, stripped the bed of its down comforter and pillow, and raced downstairs. It crossed her mind that she could be whipped for disturbing Miss Julia's bed, but she didn't care.

"Here, Mamie, this should chase off that chill," she said as she tucked it around Mamie's shaking body. "And here's a pillow for your head. Oh, wait until you see the wedding presents me and Mistress got you and Pap. For now they're a surprise. But soon, soon . . ."

Abby rattled on, trying to cheer her grandma. Mamie's mouth tightened in pain. Pulling a stool to the bedside, Abby sat and took her grandma's hand in hers. Her skin was cold and dry as paper. Her breathing was shallow. Finally, slowly, Mamie's eyes drifted shut, her shivering ceased, and she fell asleep.

Tears filled Abby's eyes. The whole trip home, she'd been dreaming of reading the *Information Wanted* and finding her Mama. Not once had she thought of Mamie. Now her grandma was surely sick. Pap was right. She was a "selfish, thoughtless chile."

Pap stole quietly into the room, his gray hair sprinkled with rain. "How is she?"

"Tired, chilled, and her chest seems to be painin' her."

"That's not a good sign. I seen too many folks die from a pain in their hearts." Pap touched Mamie's cheek.

"I wished I knowed what to do." Abby fretted. "Maybe some of Mistress's medicine would help."

Pap shook his head. "If one of us was sick, Mamie knowed what to do."

Abby sprang from the stool. "Why, Pap, *I* know what to do too. Many times I helped Mamie fix her potions and tonics. Only—only I'm not sure exactly what she needs," she admitted as she twisted her fingers together. "If the pain was outside, I'd know how to heal it. I ain sure how to heal pain on the inside."

With a sorrowful sigh, Pap sat on the stool. "Abby, there might be nothin' you can do. Sometimes it's jest a person's time to join the Lord."

"Doan say that!" Abby stuck her fingers in her ears and ran blindly into the dark kitchen. Kneeling on the hearth, she blew life into the fire. Then she lighted a candle and carried it to a cupboard. Mamie's dried roots, berries, and leaves were arranged on one shelf. Abby knew them by name, smell and curative. *But without Mamie, how will I know the right amounts? How will I know the right mixtures?*

I've got to try!

With careful thought, she selected sweet violet, ginger, and coneflower. She remembered Mamie using them for Auntie Lena, an old slave woman who'd died a summer ago. Mamie had told Abby about their ability to relieve pain and warm the blood and heart.

Only, Auntie Lena died, Abby reminded herself, worry knotting her brow as she measured the powders and leaves using pinches and spoonfuls. Then she bundled the dry mixture into a square of muslin, put it in a pot of water, and hung it over the fire to simmer. After that, she cooked up a special lavender tea for Pap and Mistress. Nursing required strength.

While waiting for the mixtures to steep, Abby retrieved the baskets from the front hall and carried them to the kitchen. The basket that held the pillows was also filled with small bags of spices to keep the wedding presents hidden from prying eyes. The second basket held sacks of flour, cornmeal, sugar, and salt, and a tin of lamp oil. As Abby unpacked, she decided that Mistress's bartering had fetched a pitiful amount of supplies. Until the garden came in, food this month would be measured in mouthfuls.

Then Abby pictured the Tuckers. When they'd stopped by the cabin on the way home, Dewey had been skinning a rat. "The onliest meat I've eaten in a week!" Little Ellie had announced excitedly.

Not that Abby hadn't eaten rat before. Skewered and roasted they were tasty. But there was scant meat to share.

Least we have a little, Abby told herself as she stocked the cupboard shelves. When she was finished, she cast about for a hiding place for the pillows. She wanted to keep them a secret until the pillow slips were sewn. But where to put them?

Upstairs in Miss Julia's room. Lately, neither Mamie nor Pap went to the second floor. Abby pulled out the pillows and then reached in the bottom of the basket for the newspaper. She knew this wasn't the right time to read the *Information Wanted*—there were folks and chores to tend to—but maybe when the house was

settled, she could dry her dress by the fire and hunt for
Mama's advertisement.

"I'm glad I found you, Abby." Mistress sailed into the
kitchen so ghostly quiet that Abby jumped a foot.

"Mistress, you startled me!" she exclaimed as she
stuffed the pillows back into the basket. "Is something
wrong?"

Mistress's eyes brimmed. "Tissie's right. Mister is out
of his head. The laudanum has calmed him, but his leg
... his leg ..." Pressing her fingers against her mouth, she
slumped into a kitchen chair. "Oh Abby, Dr. Preston said
if John's leg doesn't heal, he'll have to amputate the
entire limb." A sob escaped her lips. "And if he does, it
will be the death of my husband and the ruin of
Hammond House!"

Mister Hammond dead? Hammond House ruined? Abby
stared at Mistress. Hammond Plantation was *home.*
Where would she, Pap, Mamie, and the others go?
What would become of Mistress and this house?

Mistress dabbed her nose with a lace handkerchief.
Then she straightened her shoulders and tried to smile
cheerfully through her tears. "Pardon me for being
overly dramatic and maudlin. There is no room for
weakness when others are sick."

"Yes, Ma'am, we must stay strong." Hurrying to the
fire, Abby took the kettle off the hook and poured

Mistress a cup of the lavender tea. "Here. Drink this. It will help. Only blow on it first so you doan burn your lips."

"Thank you." Mistress took several sips and then asked, "How's Mamie?"

"Jest tired," Abby fibbed, feeling that Mistress had enough on her mind. "She'll be her old bossy self in the mornin'."

"Good. I'm glad to hear it. And I'm sorry for my tears. I'm just tired from the trip and worried about Mister Hammond."

"Mistress." Hesitant, Abby ducked her head. "I hope you'll excuse my bold words, but it seems that Dr. Preston's medicine is not going to heal Mister's leg."

Mistress sighed. "It seems you may be right. Mister Hammond has not coped well with the loss of his lower leg. What will he do when . . . ?" Her lower lip began to tremble. "However, if Dr. Preston doesn't operate and the gangrene spreads, then he will lose more than his limb. He'll lose his life. I don't think I could bear it."

"Ma'am, what if we could heal the infection? You've tried Dr. Preston's medicine. Maybe—maybe it 'bout time you tried Mamie's."

Slowly, Mistress set the mug on the table. "Abby, as an educated woman, I find it hard to believe that spells and leaves can cure ailments. However, during these past years many of my beliefs have fallen by the wayside. Even my belief in God has sorely wavered. So Abby, I will say yes to your suggestion. I am placing Mister's health in your and Mamie's hands. And I thank you for your help," she added softly, before taking her tea and leaving as quietly as she had come.

Abby fell into the vacated chair. *Oh, what have I gotten myself into? With Mamie feeling poorly, Mister's care will be solely up to me!*

A sudden breeze swirled through the kitchen, and the candle flame flickered, casting shadows on the walls. Shadows with writhing arms and legs. Abby shrank against the back of the chair as the shadows became the ghosts of Auntie Lena, Miss Julia, her Pa, and a host of neighbors, slaves, and soldiers that the war—and the years—had claimed.

Abby's head pounded with worry and fear, and she rubbed her temples. *Will the dying never end? What if I cain't heal Mister? What if Mamie gets sicker?*

Doan think about the dying! Abby chastised herself. Jumping from the chair, she marched through the shadows to the cupboard of potions. Her feet and hands were weary, but she wasn't going to let the Lord claim Mamie or Mister.

For the rest of the night, Abby worked tirelessly. She prepared a poultice of sage, figwort, and chickweed for

Mister's leg, cleaned the stump, smoothed on the poultice, and then bandaged the stump with clean strips. When Mister briefly woke, she dribbled sips of tea made from willow, elder, and cowslip down his throat. Finally, long after midnight, he drifted into a troubled sleep, and Abby rested in the rocker by the side of his bed, holding in her hands the precious newspaper she'd retrieved from the basket.

By candlelight, Abby read the *Information Wanted*. Several advertisements sparked hope, but none were from a woman named Lively. *Has Mama truly forgotten me?*

Halfway through the last column of ads, tiredness swept over her and the words blurred. She yawned deeply, her lids fluttered shut, the newspaper dropped in her lap, and she spiraled into a dreamless sleep.

The morning sun woke her. Startled, she bolted upright in the rocker. Mister Hammond was still sleeping soundly. Abby hoped it was due to the tea and healing poultice, but she knew it was partly the laudanum. Leaning over, she felt his forehead. The fever hadn't broken, but his skin felt cooler. A good sign.

Abby rose from the rocker, feeling stiff and worn. A puzzled frown creased her brow. Her lap was empty. Hadn't she gone to sleep reading the newspaper? *Perhaps it dropped to the floor.* Stooping, she hunted around the bedside table and under the bed. Then she glanced around the room, discovering no sign of it.

A chill fell over her like a dusting of frost. Unless haunts had stolen the newspaper, there was only one explanation for its disappearance. Someone had crept into the room last night and taken it. Someone who might have seen her buy it at Tate's. *Someone who doesn't want me to find Mama.*

Abby knew who that someone was—*Mistress.*

CHAPTER *Eleven*

How dare she? Abby thought, clenching her fists. *How dare she ruin my chances to find Mama!*

Tissie burst into the bedroom, her eyes red from weeping. "Abby, hurry to your grandma's side," she said without a good morning. "She callin' for you."

Fear quickly replaced Abby's anger. "What's wrong?" she asked as she hurried across the room to meet her.

Tears coursed down Tissie's cheeks. "Oh, Abby, I'm 'fraid she dyin'."

No! Pushing past Tissie, Abby raced down the steps, through the Big House, into the kitchen, and into Mamie's bedroom. Mistress and Pap were standing bedside. Pap was reading from the Bible; Mistress held a handkerchief to her lips. The resigned looks on their faces told Abby that they were saying their good-byes.

"Git out! Git out!" she screamed. "An' take your sorrowful selves with you!" Furious, she pushed at them with both hands. Startled by her outburst, Pap and Mistress scurried from the room. Abby slammed the door shut behind them, took a deep breath and turned to face Mamie.

Her grandma's skin was waxy, her body as slack as an empty potato sack. With a moan, Abby kneeled by the bedside. Placing her forehead on the mattress, she began to pray, the words tumbling wildly:

"Dear Lord in your merciful glory forgive my sins and doan take my grandma who slaved for all her years and deserves life free from woes and bondage here on this earth and not in your heaven 'cause I will not survive if you take her and . . . and . . . and . . ."

Unable to go on, Abby sobbed into the comforter. Then a hand stroked her hair and a whisper-soft voice said, "Abby, stop wailin' chile. My time is near. I ready to meet my Lord."

Abby swung her head from side to side. "No. No. You cain't give up, Mamie. I mixed a potion to heal your pain and—"

"Chile, no herb goin' to cure what ails me. I's old. So old I doan even knowed when I's born. Freedom. Gittin' married. All dat happiness plum wore dis old body out."

Her fingers trailed lightly down Abby's cheek to her chin. "Look at me, chile."

Abby raised her head. Mamie was lying on her side and her bright eyes held Abby's. "I want you to promise one thing. You promise to keep learnin'. You growin' up in freedom, Abby. Dat's a chance I never got. I doan wants you to spend your life slavin' like me."

"I promise, Mamie."

Mamie smiled dreamily as if her thoughts were far away. "I may not knowed when I's born, but I remember your birth. Oh, your mama scream and carry on and den in a blink of an eye you was here and I held you and it was de happiest moment of my life."

"And now you cain't leave me, Mamie. Who gonna love me? Who I gonna love back?"

"You gots lots of folks to love. Mistress, Pap, Tissie, Cyril, Zee—dey your family." Mamie closed her eyes and then whispered, "And, Abby, you also have you Mama."

Abby clutched the comforter. "My Mama?"

"Fo' I die . . . I need to tell you . . . the story of Lively." Mamie's words grew faint.

"Mamie, you doan need to tell me 'bout Mama," Abby insisted. "I doan care no more. I jest want you well." She held her breath, waiting, but her grandma did-n't respond. Placing her hand in front of Mamie's lips, she felt a puff of air on her palm. Relieved, she plopped her forehead back on the comforter and again prayed.

Her grandma slept. Slowly, Abby rose and quietly left the room. Pap sat in the kitchen chair, the Bible open in front of him. Tissie was stirring a pot hanging over the fire. Cyril sat on a stool at the counter chopping potatoes. They all cast anxious glances toward Abby. No one said a word.

Abby cleared her throat. "She sleepin'."

"Good. Good." Tissie bobbed her head. "Den she not in pain. I's makin' beef broth. When she wakes, I'll see if she'll sip some."

Without replying, Abby walked over to the table. The newspaper was by Pap's arm. Frowning, she glanced from the paper to Pap, who wouldn't meet her eyes.

"You took it?"

"Yes, I did."

"Why?"

"'Cause I knowed your grandma was ill, chile. And I didn't want you talkin' of findin' your Ma and leavin' here. I didn't want you breakin' Mamie's already ailin' heart."

Abby sighed. "Have I bin that selfish?"

Pap chuckled. "Stubborn more like it."

"Too stubborn to let Mamie die," Abby declared as she squared her shoulders. "I gots more healin' potion.

I's goin' to sit vigil all night. Cyril, you have to feed the hogs for me. Tissie you help Mistress with Mister. His poultice in the crock on the counter. The Lord ain takin' Mamie without a fight!"

❊ ❊ ❊

That night, Abby rested on the floor by Mamie's bed. She'd dragged her pallet from Miss Julia's room and laid it by the bedside. Earlier, Mamie had swallowed some potion but only on Abby's insistence. She wouldn't touch the beef tea.

"Abby."

Abby bolted from the pallet. Her grandma's eyes were closed but her hand was outstretched, reaching for her. Abby took it in hers. "What, Mamie?"

"Set here by me and listen. I ready to tell your Mama's story."

"You sure you got the strength?"

"I needs to do it 'fore I die."

You ain goin' to die! Abby wanted to shout. Only suddenly, *horribly*, she wasn't so sure. Carefully, she perched on the edge of the bed. Her grandma grasped her hand tightly.

"Elizabeth was her born name," Mamie began, her voice weak. "But we called her Lively 'cause she spunkier den a frisky filly. When we first came to work at Hammond Plantation, she caught the eye of all the men. Only she had her eye on jest one—Gabe, your pa. Gabe was as handsome as he was proud, and a fine blacksmith, and he got along fine with Master Hammond 'cause Master was fair. But when Kennedy came dere was trouble."

"Kennedy the overseer?" Abby asked, remembering him from Tissie's and Zee's stories.

Mamie nodded. "Dat be him. Man meaner den Satan."

"Is that why Pa ran away? 'Cause Kennedy whipped him?"

"De truth colder and harder den a whippin'." Mamie pressed her palm against her chest and Abby bit her lip anxiously. "Mamie, is your heart painin' you?"

"No, chile. Dese sad memories are."

"Then stop," Abby demanded. "I doan want the past killin' you!"

"Past been bottled up too long, chile. It's time it was told. So hush now and let me speak." After taking a shaky breath, Mamie began again. "Master gave his consent, and Gabe and Lively married, and your Mama soon grew big with chile. Gabe worked hard and did like Master Hammond asked, but he wouldn't obey Kennedy. That made Kennedy powerful mad, and he schemed to git your Pa." Mamie's face turned troubled and Abby squeezed her fingers. "One day when Master

Hammond went to town Kennedy caught your Pa alone. He knocked Gabe cold and began to whip him bloody. When your Mama saw, she ran up screamin', Kennedy threw her down ... and ... whipped ... her ... too."

Mamie's voice faded, and she closed her eyes as if exhausted. Abby caught her breath, picturing the horrible scene. She remembered how scared she'd been when the patroller had cracked his whip. Yet that was nothing compared to the terror Gabe and Lively must have felt!

Mamie's eyelids fluttered, and she opened her mouth as if trying to speak.

"Here." Abby held up the cup of tea, but her grandma pushed her hand away.

"I needs to tell dis, chile. When your Pa saw Kennedy whip Lively, he went mad." Mamie hesitated, and raising her eyes to the ceiling, said, "Forgive me, Lord," before continuing. "Gabe grabbed Kennedy off your Mama and killed him with his bare hands. By dat time, I'd run out to help Lively. Her back was torn and bleeding. She was clutchin' her swollen belly. Jest den Master Hammond came home. Gabe stood tall and told Master what he'd done. Master didn't blame Gabe for protectin' his wife, so he gave Gabe food and money and told him to run away so the law wouldn't hang him."

"What about Mama?"

"Lively cried to go with him. But her skin was cut to shreds and she was near to birthin' you. Your Pa had no choice but to run." Sighing wearily, Mamie struggled to turn onto her back. "We buried dat no good Kennedy in de woods. Den Master and me made up a story to tell slaves and whites alike. Oh, but we told everyone dat Gabe run away to keep from bein' whipped. We told everyone dat when Gabe run off, Kennedy whipped Lively in revenge, and dat when Master found out, he run Kennedy off de farm. It was a lie we kept in our hearts to dis day."

"But, Mamie, what about Lively? Why did she leave?"

"De next day, after all dis horror, you was born, a tiny wrinkled babe. Lively was weak from loss of blood. And she was grievin' for your Pa, so I cared for you. Den as soon as Lively could walk, she ran away to find Gabe."

"And left me behind!" Abby cried. "How could my Mama abandon me, her own child?"

Mamie patted her hand. "Doan be too hard on your Mama. She was young and scared. And she knew she'd never find your Pa with a babe in her arms."

"Did she ever find him? Before he died?"

Mamie shook her head. "I doan know. Slave catchers shot Gabe when he tried to cross de border into Maryland. Dey brought his body back, thinkin' there was reward, and we buried him in de cemetery. I never heard from your Mama again."

"Oh, Mamie, why couldn't you tell me this before?" Abby laid her head on Mamie's quilt-covered belly. "I would have kept the secret too."

"Chile, I couldn't. When I was a slave, I couldn't tell 'cause Master Hammond threatened to sell you away from me if I did. Forgive me Lord, but Master was scared: He'd covered up a white man's death and let the killer, a slave, go free. As you got older, I didn't wan' to tell 'cause I knowed how it would hurt you when you found out your Mama left you. And I also couldn't tell 'cause . . ." She stopped talking, and Abby tilted her chin to look at her. Her grandma was wiping her eyes with the back of her hand. "'Cause I a selfish old woman who didn't want to lose you to your Mama."

Abby rose up. "You woan lose me, Mamie. Ever. Now rest."

Mamie smiled tiredly, and when she dozed, Abby let her tears fall. Tears for her Pa who'd had to kill a man to defend his wife and then was killed running for freedom. Tears for her Mama who'd left her babe in search of her husband. Tears for Mamie who'd lost a daughter to a terrible secret. And tears for herself because Mamie was right; all her life she'd dreamed of her Mama, but never had her Mama abandoned her in her dreams.

Which means that Mama ain lookin' for me—and never has been!

Now she had no dream.

"Chile."

Abby glanced down at Mamie. Her face was ashen and although she was trying to speak, her lips were barely moving. Heart heavy, Abby leaned over to listen. "I also never tol' you 'bout your Mama cause I swore on the Bible dat I'd keep . . ." Mamie's voice faded, and Abby moved closer ". . . dat I'd keep Mistress's secret."

Mistress's secret? Abby reared back, wondering if she'd heard right. "What does Mistress have to do with Mama?"

Mamie beckoned her nearer. *"Look in Mistress's heart,"* she choked out, and then her grip loosened and her head fell to the side.

"Mamie?" Abby gently shook Mamie's shoulder. "Mamie?" Her grandma's chest rose faintly under the comforter, but when there was no response, Abby knew that soon the Lord would be embracing her beloved grandma. "Pap, Tissie, Mistress!" she called over her shoulder, her cry thick with tears. "Come quick!"

❋ ❋ ❋

Abby stared at the mound of fresh dirt, then kneeled and laid a bouquet of violets and daisies below the wooden cross. For two days they'd chanted and sang over Mamie's carefully washed and wrapped body. Then they'd buried her with her head to the west so she could greet the angel Gabriel when he sounded his trumpet.

Abby knew that her grandma was walking—no, *skipping*—to Heaven, and that it was time to say good-bye. She just wished her heart didn't ache so. "I'll miss you always, Mamie," she whispered.

Rising, she walked to her Pa's gravesite, long over-grown with Queen Anne's lace and pokeweed. The wooden cross listed, and she righted it with her hand. A lump rose in her throat, but she didn't cry. After three days, there were no more tears.

Even her soul felt painfully empty.

Abby knew that she had Pap, Tissie, Cyril, Mistress, and the others to care for and love, but her blood kin were all dead. *Unless Mama's still alive.* But Mamie claimed she'd never heard from her daughter. And if her Pa once knew the secret of Lively, he had long ago taken it to his grave.

Abby walked from the slave section of the cemetery to Miss Julia's grave, marked by a headstone that read: BORN APRIL 16, 1855. DIED DECEMBER 4, 1864.

Mistress had bartered dearly for the stone, which was etched with angels and flowers. "I miss you, too, Miss Julia," Abby said as she traced her finger over the simple inscription: *She brought love and laughter to our lives.*

Which is how her grandma had described Lively.

With Mamie dead, Abby knew she'd have to be satisfied with the story her grandma had left her. She'd have to accept that she'd never find out the whole truth of her Mama. *Unless Mistress . . .*

Abby shook her head. Right now, Mistress was mourning, too. There was no way Abby could poke and pry old memories. She'd have to be patient.

Sometimes, Abby thought as she placed the last bundle of wildflowers below the child's headstone, *life is as burdensome as endless chores.*

She hoped that Mamie would find days of happiness in Heaven.

✳ ✳ ✳

CHAPTER *Twelve*

"Abby," Tissie said as she stirred the pot of boiling wash water. Abby glanced up from her clothes sorting. Tissie's eyes were gleaming and she couldn't hide her smile. "I know it's only ten days since your grandma's death. But me and Zee wants to git married. Only we wants to ask your permission since the farm still in mournin'."

Abby dropped the armful of dirty drawers. "Oh Tissie! It would make me happy to see you and Zee wed." Wrapping her arms around her friend's bony ribs, she gave her a hug. "Make Mamie happy too. She be lookin' down from Heaven with a smile on her face. Oh, and now that the garden comin' in we can fix a feast for all. Maybe even a weddin' cake!"

Tissie's grin dimpled her round cheeks. "Thank you.

I tell Zee tonight when he comes in from de fields."

"A weddin'!" Abby repeated as she finished tossing the underclothes into the steaming pot. Since her grandma's death, Abby and Tissie had taken over the cooking as well as the cleaning. A wedding would help take Abby's mind off her sorrowful thoughts and swollen feet.

"Mistress be excited too," Abby added. "'Specially now that Mister gettin' well."

Tissie humphed. "Mister's healin' no thanks to Doctor Preston, and all thanks to you and Mamie's potions."

"And Mistress's nursin'," Abby reminded her. "She ain left his bedside since we buried Mamie."

"You doan need to tell me," Tissie grumbled as she heaved a wet mass of clothes from the wash pot into the rinse water. "We be doin' all the work while she doin' all the mournin.'"

"She took Mamie's death hard," Abby admitted, glancing toward the Big House. "Some nights I hear her weepin' for hours. Maybe that make her determined not to lose Mister, too."

Tissie humphed again. "Seems we in mournin' and still find time to cook and clean," she complained, and Abby burst out laughing.

Tissie propped her fists on her hips. "What so funny?"

"You sound jest like Mamie," Abby explained. "Sometimes I think her soul done set up house in your body."

"Dat fine with me as long as she doin' her share of de work," Tissie said, making Abby laugh even harder.

When the washing was done Abby headed to the garden to pick peas. She spotted Pap's hoe propped up against the picket fence, but there was no sign of her grandpa. *Probably gone fishin' with Cyril*, Abby figured. Every afternoon, the two stole off to the stream with their poles. Abby didn't dare scold even though the weeds and squash bugs were taking over the garden. Mamie's death had stolen Pap's spunk, and fishing was one of the few things that brought him joy.

Abby sighed as she bent over the row of peas. The sun beat down on her back, which already ached from the hours of stirring, hanging, and sorting. But at least she wasn't in the fields.

Only a handful of men remained to work the crops, and they labored long and hard. "We still work all day," Zee told her when she asked about the difference between slave and free. "But at night we do as we please."

Which reminded Abby it was time she got back to her nights of reading and writing. Straightening, she rubbed the small of her back, remembering her promise to her grandma to keep learning. *Oh, Mamie, why did you have to leave me? Why did you have to die when you was jest tastin' freedom?*

Didn't seem the Lord was fair.

When the basket was full, Abby picked up the hoe. As she chopped the weeds around the potato plants, her thoughts drifted back to the night Mamie had died. Her grandma's story was all she had left of her Mama, and she vowed not to forget it. Every day, she recalled the tale of Kennedy, Gabe, and Lively. How Kennedy beat Gabe and then raised the whip to Lively and—

Suddenly, Abby shot upright.

"When your Pa saw Kennedy whip Lively, he went mad," Mamie had said, but then she'd hesitated, raised her eyes to the ceiling, and said, *"Forgive me, Lord,"* before adding, *"Gabe grabbed Kennedy off your Ma and killed him with his bare hands."*

Abby clamped a sweaty palm to her mouth. Mamie always said, *"Forgive me Lord,"* whenever she told a lie. That could only mean one thing—Gabe hadn't killed Kennedy!

But how could that be? Wasn't it the reason Gabe ran away? And if Gabe hadn't killed Kennedy, then who had?

Or was Mamie's entire story a lie?

Abby whacked the dirt around the turnip tops.

Mamie said she'd kept silent for thirteen years because she was sparing Abby's feelings. But who was she really sparing? And why did she lie?

"I also never told you 'bout your Mama cause I swore on the Bible dat I'd keep Mistress's secret."

Abby stopped chopping. *Mistress.*

Mistress who fainted whenever Abby spoke of Lively.

Mistress who was hoarding secrets about the past too. Only Mamie had never once mentioned Mistress's name in her whole tale. What part had Mistress played in the tragedy? *What is her secret!*

Look in Mistress's heart.

Abby recalled Mamie's last words. Mamie had to know that Mistress would never share with Abby the secrets locked in her heart. So what was she speaking about?

Might be I'll never know! Frustrated, Abby gave the weeds one last thrashing. Then dropping the hoe, she picked up the basket of peas and headed for the kitchen. Supper needed to be fixed. Questions would have to wait for hungry folks.

❋ ❋ ❋

After supper, Abby fixed a steaming bowl of beef tea for Mister Hammond. Carefully, she carried it up the slave stairway and down the upstairs hall. As she passed Mistress's room, a noise made her glance inside.

Mistress stood in front of her chifforobe. Bent over, she was lifting something from the lower drawers. Abby caught a glimpse of a wooden box, and she gripped the bowl tightly when she realized what it was:

Mistress's heart-shaped jewelry box.

What if Mamie hadn't been talking about Mistress's *real* heart?

Afraid that Mistress might see her, Abby scurried past the doorway, spilling tea on the hall floor. Her heart began beating furiously. Mistress kept the jewelry box hidden, so Abby had only seen it once or twice. Abby thought it was because Mistress was afraid someone might steal the last of her jewelry. But was she really hiding the truth about Lively?

One thing was certain, Abby *had* to find out. The heart-shaped box might hold the answer to her questions.

Breathless, Abby hurried into Mister's bedroom. He was propped up on two pillows, and his eyes tracked her approach as she crossed the floor.

"Good evenin', Mister Hammond," Abby greeted him. Although the fever had broken days ago and clean flesh covered his stump, she was never quite sure how Mister would respond. Sometimes he thought he was still on the battlefield. Sometimes he thought she was Mistress or Julia.

He frowned as if puzzled. "Are you the same nurse I had yesterday? I don't recall you."

Abby set the bowl on the side table. "Sometimes Mistress or Tissie. . . ."

"And what did the doctor do to my leg?" he asked, angrily thumping the mattress below his knee. "I told Dr. Rush not to amputate. I told him I'd take my chances. I told him that a man with a missing limb is an abomination!"

Abby bit her lip, realizing that Mister's mind was back in the field hospital where he'd been taken after he was shot. "Sir, I'm Abby. You at Hammond House, your home, where you was born."

Mister gazed at her in disbelief. Slowly, the anger drained from his gaunt face. "I'm at Hammond House?"

"You bin here since March. Almost three months."

"Three months? How can that be? Just yesterday I was on the battlefield commanding my men—" He leaned forward, agitated. "The *war*, my God. Is the war still going on?"

Abby hesitated, not sure what to say. Had his mind finally returned? And if it had, could he handle the news of the South's defeat? "I believe you need to talk to Mistress Hammond. There's so much to tell an' I doan rightly know where to start." She gestured toward the doorway. "She in her room. I can call her."

He sank back against the pillows. "Don't disturb her yet."

"You need some nourishment, too, sir." Abby picked up the bowl.

He cut his eyes toward her. "Abby, tell me about Julia."

Abby blanched. "Oh, Mister Hammond. I—I—"

"I know she died. That I will *never* forget. And I know the entire plantation mourned her. What *I* want to hear is stories of when she was alive! When I left for the war, I missed so much of her life."

Abby raised the bowl. Dipping a spoon into the broth, she held it toward his mouth. "Suppose I talk while you eat?"

Minutes later, Mistress walked in. Halfway across the room, she stopped and stared at her husband.

"Hello, Rebecca," Mister said with a trace of a smile.

"John?" Mistress choked out, and running to the other side of the bed, she threw herself in her husband's arms.

Abby sprang from the bed. "If you doan need me, I'll help Tissie in the kitchen." Setting the bowl on the bedside table, she hurried into the hall, only one thought on her mind: *Now's my chance to find the jewelry box!*

Without hesitation, she ran into Mistress's bedroom, carefully closing the door behind her.

The doors to the chifforobe were closed. Abby

opened them, revealing Mistress's robes and shawls neatly hanging from hooks. Kneeling, Abby opened the lower drawer and carefully searched through the folded underclothes and stockings. There was no jewelry box.

Mistress must have moved it!

Frustrated, Abby sat back on her heels. Her gaze lighted on the trunk at the foot of the bed. Was the jewel box inside? Abby hoped it wasn't locked.

The lid lifted easily. Inside, Mistress's gowns and fine dresses were stacked in piles. They were folded neatly and covered with protective sleeves of muslin. Mistress hadn't worn her finery in years, and dried flower petals were sprinkled on top to keep away moths and mildew.

Abby hunted through the gowns. At the bottom, under a velour traveling coat, she found the heart-shaped box.

She pulled it out, her stomach tight with worry— with *anticipation*. If there was only jewelry inside, it would mean the end of her search for Lively.

She raised the lid. There were no cameos, brooches or diamonds. Only a stack of letters secured with ribbon.

Heart thumping, Abby slipped a letter from the stack and unfolded it. It was dated February 1859, two years before the war. *Dear Mistress Rebecca*, the letter began. Impatient, Abby skimmed to the closing at the bottom of the page.

Yurs in faith,
Elizabeth Joyner

Abby caught her breath and a small joyful sound escaped her. It was from her Mama! Mamie had been right about the heart-shaped box!

Scooting out of sight behind the bed, she hungrily read the letter.

Febuary 2, 1859

Dear Mistress Rebecca,
I is finale safe. I is living in the state of Pennsylvania with a Quaker famlee named Parker. I works for them by day. At night I go to school. Tell Mamie I am ready to kare for Abby. I miss her so! Why have you not replid to my prevous letters? Pleeze reply to the addres below and tell me when and where we kin meet so I can bring her to live with me in Pennsylvania. I promis that yur secret is safe with me. I only want Abby to grow up free. Give my lov to her. Tell her I miss her with al my soul.

Yurs in faith,
Elizabeth Joyner.

Overcome, Abby pressed the letter to her chest. *Mama didn't abandon me!* Again she checked the date. It was written when she was eight years old. Had her Mama written before then as well? Were all these her letters?

Untying the ribbon, she shuffled through the letters, nine in all, checking the dates. There was one for every year until the war started. With shaking fingers, Abby unfolded the earliest letter, dated 1852, the year her Mama had left Hammond House. This time the writing and spelling were perfect, and Abby knew someone must have written it for her.

November 1852

Dear Mrs. Rebecca Hammond,
I am writing for one Elizabeth Joyner, eighteen years old, who was your slave. She has escaped to Pennsylvania where she is currently residing with our family. When she came to us, she was perilously close to death. I nursed her back to health, but lately she has been despondent over the death of her husband and the decision to leave her child, Abigail, behind. She wishes to be reunited with Abigail; however, we have advised her not to travel to Virginia since she will be returned to bondage. Please reply so we can discuss her wishes. However, please keep her whereabouts a secret. We are fearful that she might be returned to slavery. Elizabeth assures us that you are an educated, compassionate woman who would not deny her this request.

Sincerely,
Mrs. Patrick Graham

Abby felt lightheaded, as if her soul had been freed. Not only had Mama *not* abandoned her, she'd been looking for her for years! Oh, why hadn't Mistress shown her the letters?

Abby hunted through the other letters; the last one was dated 1860. Had something happened to her Mama then? Or had the letters ceased due to the war?

A thump accompanied by loud voices startled her.

"She's here. I know she's here!" she heard Mister John holler.

"No, John, you must go back to bed," Mistress replied. "Your limb is only now healing. The new flesh is fragile."

Abby peeked around the bedpost. The thumps and voices grew louder. Master and Mistress were in the hallway beyond the closed door. If they came in, they'd find her snooping in the bedroom.

Abby hadn't been given permission to go through Mistress's things; she could be accused of stealing.

A deathly chill came over her.

Slaves had been hung for less!

* * *

CHAPTER *Thirteen*

Scrambling to her knees, Abby tossed the letters in the trunk and closed the lid. Then she belly-crawled under Mistress's bed. An instant later the door crashed open and Mister hobbled into the bedroom.

Abby held her breath.

"She's in here, Rebecca," Mister insisted, his voice hoarse. "Our daughter's in here!"

"Please, John, come back to bed," Mistress pleaded.

"Not until I see Julia!"

From under the bed, Abby watched Mister's bare foot and the tip of his crutch cross the floor, Mistress's skirts switching behind him.

Abby grimaced. She'd left the doors to the chifforobe open. They'd spot her for sure!

"Look, John, she's not here," Mistress was saying. "Julia's safe in Heaven. Why, I bet she's with Mamie right now, and they're picking a bouquet of flowers for—"

"But I heard her," Mister protested, sounding unsure.

"And I did, too," Mistress said gently. "The truth is that every minute of every day, I hear her. Remember the song she loved so dearly? Hush Little Baby . . ." she began to sing, and slowly the two moved back across the floor and out the door.

Abby heaved a sigh as she shimmied from under the bed. *Thank goodness Mister Hammond thought I was Julia's ghost!*

Standing, she brushed the dust off her dress. Then she snorted with disdain at her earlier fear. *I shouldn't be scared of Mistress anymore,* she told herself. *I ain no slave. And I got a Mama who wants me!*

The letters proved it.

Abby glanced at the door to make sure it was closed and then kneeled again before the trunk. The letters weren't addressed to her so she couldn't rightly take them. But she could commit her Mama's words to heart. Even more important, she could find the address on the last letter so she could reply.

Then my dream will surely come true!

She opened the trunk and was reaching in for the letters when a hand gripped her shoulder. Abby squeaked. She didn't need to turn her head to know who was behind her.

"I knew you had to be Julia's ghost," Mistress said, her voice tremulous. "I knew you wouldn't let up searching for your mother."

"And I found her too!" Abby said. Twisting from Mistress's grasp, she jumped to her feet. "I found her in these letters. Letters you kept from me all these years." She waved them in Mistress's face. "Oh, why didn't you let me go to her! You had no right to keep me from my Mama all these years."

With a cry of distress, Mistress crumpled under Abby's accusation. Sinking onto the mattress, she placed her head in her hands. Abby wasn't swayed. Mistress had been keeping the secret too long.

"I knew it was time to show you the letters," Mistress said from between her fingers. "Earlier, when I took out the box, I told myself it was time you knew the truth." She peered up. "I just didn't know where to start."

"What's going on here?"

Abby whirled around to see Mister Hammond standing in the doorway, propped on one crutch. Mistress leaped to her feet. "John, you should be in bed."

"Not until I find out what's going on!" Swaying unsteadily, he fell against the door frame.

Mistress hurried over to him. "Abby and I were just

discussing the past," she told him, her cheeks flushed. "I've—I've decided it's time we told her the truth," she added hesitantly.

Puzzlement filled Mister's eyes. "The truth?"

Gently, Mistress took his elbow. "Yes, you remember the incident that happened long before the war. It was when Gabe, Kennedy, and Lively lived at Hammond Plantation," she explained as she led him into the hall. Before leaving, she glanced over her shoulder at Abby. Her eyes were red-rimmed. "Abby saved your life, you know. Her medicine healed your fever and your leg. It's time we repay her with the truth. However, right now, she's going to fix some of her special tea. And then we'll talk."

Astonished by the unexpected turn of events, Abby watched them go. Then she looked longingly at the letters still clenched in her hand.

Had she heard right? Was Mistress going to tell her what happened?

Am I finally going to know the truth? Abby wondered as she carefully, *reverently*, placed her Mama's letters in the trunk and hurried from the bedroom.

❋ ❋ ❋

"When I came to Hammond Plantation, I was young, spoiled, and haughty," Mistress began her story. She and Abby were at the kitchen table sipping lavender tea.

Exhausted from his earlier ordeal, Mister had fallen asleep after drinking his healing potion.

Mistress sat across from Abby, her face composed. A single candle glowed between them. "My father had given me everything, and after I married John, he denied me nothing. Still, the isolation of the farm drove me out of my mind. Living in Staunton at the seminary, I was used to days and evenings of lectures, music, and discourse. When I moved to Nelson County, I was alone except for John. Lively, your mother, became my personal servant. However, she soon became more than that." A smile softened her face. "We were almost the same age, and she became my friend and confidant. It was she who made life tolerable with her laughter."

As Mistress spoke, Abby listened intently, afraid to miss a word. All her life, she'd been waiting for this story.

"I was jealous when she fell in love with Gabe, your father," Mistress continued, gazing into her cup. "However, I encouraged their marriage, seeing it as a way to keep Lively at Hammond House forever. You see, your mother desperately wanted to be free. Although she never expressed it to me, I often heard her and Mamie arguing about it." Mistress glanced up at Abby. "You two were alike in that matter."

"Do I look like my Mama?" Abby asked.

Mistress tilted her head, studying her. "You look more like your father, but you have your mother's spirit. Anyway, I reasoned that marriage and babies would bind her forever to Hammond House—and, more importantly, to me. And I was right. After Lively married, she was content. Until the night Kennedy was killed."

Mistress fell silent and a cloud darkened her face. Abby stiffened. She'd already heard the story once from Mamie, but just the mention of Kennedy sent goosebumps up her arms. "That was the night Kennedy whipped my Ma almost to death."

Mistress nodded. Grief creased her brow and she pressed her lips together as if to hold back her emotions. "Gabe refused to run away unless Lively went with him," she finally went on. "However, your mother was in no condition. She was bleeding from the beating and about to give birth. John knew that if Gabe didn't run, he'd be lynched. He agreed to send Lively to him after you were born. However, things didn't work out. Gabe left, you were born, and Lively quickly recovered. John made arrangements to have her join your pa." Mistress lowered her eyes. "Only I refused to let her go."

Abby's lips parted. Slowly, she set down her cup. *This is a part of the story I've never heard.*

"I told John I couldn't bear life without her. I begged

and cajoled, thinking only of my own selfish needs, and John gave in to my pleas. He told your mother she had to stay. Lively was heartbroken. She refused to speak to me, knowing I was the reason she couldn't join her husband. I was just as stubborn. *She will come around,* I reasoned. *She'll realize this was the best choice.* The next day, she was gone."

Sighing deeply, Mistress laced her fingers around the cup.

"Leaving me with Mamie," Abby said.

Mistress looked up sharply. "Don't blame her for that. Blame me. If I'd allowed John to make the arrangements, you would have gone with Lively. She never wanted to leave you behind. I forced her to make that choice." Tears shimmered in her eyes. "And I was so angry when she did! *Furious.* How could she choose Gabe over me? That's what went through my foolish, frivolous head." Reaching over, Mistress covered Abby's hand with hers.

Abby tensed, wanting to recoil from her touch. *You sent my Mama away!* she wanted to shout, but the pain glimmering in Mistress's eyes hushed her accusation.

"Oh, Abby, I shudder at my behavior. When Gabe was killed and the patrollers brought him back to Hammond House, I secretly *exalted,* believing that Lively would quickly return to me. When she didn't return, I grew even angrier. *How could she choose freedom over me?* I thought. Oh, can you imagine my selfishness? I am ashamed to look back at the spoiled person I was. I had no idea what freedom meant. I had no idea what it felt like to lose someone you loved."

Abby slid her hand from under Mistress's. "But soon you did. Why then did you keep the letters from me?"

Mistress looked away as if ashamed. "When Lively first wrote, I was too angry to reply. From her letters I knew that she was constantly moving, trying to keep away from the slave hunters. I reasoned there was no way she could care for a child. At least that's what I told myself, but if I had searched my soul, I would have discovered that I was really keeping you from her as *punishment* for her running away. Later, when I had Julia, and my heart grew less selfish, I realized how deeply I had hurt your mother. And how much she must miss you. I was stricken with guilt at what I'd done. By then she was settled, and her letters were no less beseeching in her wish to be reunited with you."

"You could have tol' me 'bout her then," Abby accused. "You could have tol' me how much she loved me."

Mistress dropped her gaze. "You're right. And I am ashamed that I didn't. However, by then, everyone at Hammond House loved you, including my daughter.

You were only six when she was born, but when you held Julia in your arms, she'd gurgle and coo happily." Mistress smiled at the memory. "I realize that's no excuse. But you had a wonderful life with Mamie and Pap and you seemed content. I also was afraid that if you left Mamie would grieve herself to death. Then the war came, and the letters stopped, and I didn't hear from Lively—until the day we went to Tomasford."

Abby leaped from the chair, almost upsetting it. "You got another letter from my Mama?"

Reaching inside her collar, Mistress pulled an envelope from her bodice. "I've been carrying it next to my heart, trying to decide what to do."

Look in Mistress's heart. Is that what Mamie had meant? Did her grandma suspect that Mistress had picked up a letter the day they went to town?

"I didn't open it, Abby. It's addressed to you. I didn't give it to you right away because I wanted to speak to Mamie first. Then she got sick and I never got the chance."

Fingers shaking, Abby took the letter.

Rising, Mistress picked up her cup. "I'll leave you alone with it," she said, and left without another word.

Abby tore open the envelope. Several paper bills fell onto the tabletop. Too anxious to stop and count the money, Abby pulled out the letter:

May 4, 1865

My darling Abigail,

The long war is over and I trust this letter will find you and Mamie in freedom. I have written over the years, but I believe the turmoil in the country has kept my letters from reaching you. Hopefully, this will find you all in good health. Oh, how I have missed you! I try and picture what you look like. Are you as handsome as your father? But enough sentiment. I have enclosed money for your and Mamie's train fare. I want you to join me in Pennsylvania. Now that all slaves are free, there should be no laws to hold you in Virginia. I work in a millinery store and rent a small cottage. It is not large, but I want you and Mamie to live with me here. My heart will not rest until I am reunited with my family! Tell Mistress Hammond that the past should hold us in bondage no longer. We must put the memories of Kennedy's shooting behind us and begin anew. Lastly, tell Mistress Rebecca I forgive her. Please reply as soon as possible. I have never stopped loving you, dear Abigail.

Yours in Faith,
Elizabeth Joyner

Tears dripped on the page. Crushing the letter to her chest, Abby grabbed the candleholder and ran from the kitchen into the night. She had to tell Mamie the news!

All this time, Lively had never forgotten either of them. And now she wanted them to come live with her.

Ma, in her own cottage!

Stumbling blindly in the dark, Abby almost lost the candle and the letter. When she reached the edge of the cemetery, she stopped in confusion, trying to make sense of where she was. The trees, crosses, and head-stones looked ghostly in the flickering candlelight.

Finally, she spotted the mound of Mamie's grave. She tread carefully, afraid of tripping and falling. Afraid of—

A black shape seemed to cover the grave. Abby's mouth went dry. She held the candle high, but a gust of wind snuffed out the flame.

Ain no such things as haunts, Abby told herself. Her knees shook. Licking her dry lips, she made her way through the weeds. She wasn't about to let any spirit chase her away from Mamie's grave. There was too much news to tell her.

The black shape rose from beside the mound, stopping Abby cold in her tracks. "Abby?" a voice called. "That you, chile?"

Abby heaved a sigh. "Pap! You like to scare me to death."

"You like to scare *me* to death! What you doin' out here?"

"What *you* doin' out here?" Abby asked as she came

up to him. He'd spread several sacks next to the grave, balling up one for a pillow.

Sitting up, Pap clasped his hands around his knees. "Well, it's like this. For eleven years I slept beside your grandma. Now I cain't sleep in that bed without her."

Abby laughed. "Oh, Pap." She sat down beside him. "You cain't keep sleepin' outside on the ground. Your gout will get you and we'll have to hitch Toby to your arms to pull you up."

"You tell Mamie that." Pap patted the mound of dirt beside him. "She keeps callin' me to come out and sleep by her side."

"Pap, Mamie in heaven. She's not in this cold ground." Abby took his hand in hers.

"I knows that chile. My mind ain that addled. It just goin' to take me awhile to git used to nights without her."

Abby squeezed his fingers. "Are you ready for some good news, Pap? Oh, there's so much to tell I doan know where to start."

"You mean 'bout Tissie and Zee gittin' married? I already decided to give them the new bed we ordered for their weddin' present."

Abby nodded. "There's that news. And there's Mister's mind clearin'. It was like he finally woke from a long sleep. Now he knows where he is!"

Pap swatted his leg and cackled with glee. "Thank the Lord. And thank you, Mamie." He again patted the ground. "Abby used your tonics to finally mend that man. Now we kin git this farm bountiful again."

"But I saved the best news for last." Abby pressed the letter into his hand. "It's a letter from my Mama. From Lively!"

Pap's jaw dropped.

"She been writin' me for twelve years. Mistress been hidin' the letters in her jewelry box. Oh, doan ask me why. The story too tangled. Do you want me to read it? I'll read it out loud so Mamie can hear, too." Without waiting for a reply, Abby opened the letter and read. When she was finished, she gave Pap's skinny shoulders a hug. "I'm writing to her tonight. Soon as she replies, I'm packin' up and leavin'. She even sent some money. Oh, I've never been to Pennsylvania. Doesn't it sound grand?"

Still Pap didn't speak. Abby turned to look at him. His face was hidden in the shadows, but his eyes glimmered.

"Oh Pap. Doan be sad. You can come with me. Lively will love you as much as I do."

He wiped his eyes. "No, chile. I needs to stay here with Mamie. I'm jest cryin' 'cause I'm overjoyed for you. You finally found your Mama."

"I finally did." Abby snuggled against his side, thinking about all that had happened. *Overjoyed.* Pap had used the right word. That's what she was feeling. Except for a few thorns of sadness poking her heart. "An Pap, leavin' isn't forever," she whispered as she pressed against him. "I'll come back and visit. *I promise.*"

※ ※ ※

CHAPTER *Fourteen*

The next day, Abby sat at the desk in the parlor, her Mama's letters spread in front of her. Last night, she'd read each one over and over, memorizing special lines. *I have never stopped loving you, dear Abigail. I miss you with all my soul. My life has been barren without you, my beloved child.* Those words had warmed her through the sleepless night.

Now she sat, pen in hand, poised to reply. Writing paper was dear, so she couldn't afford to make mistakes. But expressing thirteen years of longing on one page seemed a hopeless task.

Dipping the pen in ink, she began: *Dearest Mama,*
Then she paused. *Oh, what do I write next!*
Should I gush on and on about how much I've missed her?

Or should I keep it polite?

Neither seemed suitable.

Sighing, Abby slumped in the desk chair. Mistress's voice drifted down the stairs. She was in Mister's bedroom, discussing crops, freed slaves, and the war's end. Mister had months to catch up on. Abby and Mama had *years*. It made her heart joyful. It made her head ache.

Cyril tiptoed into the room carrying a feather duster. Keeping his eyes on Abby, he swished it in the air.

"Cyril," Abby said impatiently. "Are you dustin' or spyin'?"

"Spyin'," Cyril said without hesitation. Hurrying over, he tapped one of the letters. "Read it to me, Abby. I wants to hear all 'bout your Mama. I wants to hear 'bout the Quakers. What are Quakers?"

"Folks who doan believe in war or slaves."

"Tell me 'bout dem an' 'bout the millenary shop. What's millenary?"

Abby giggled. "Cyril, you as curious as a blue jay. I believe you need to read them yourself."

"You know I cain read."

"Well, it's time you learned. Mistress can teach you."

He snorted. "I doan need to read and write to catch possum and eel."

"That's all you gonna do the rest of your life?"

"Yes 'um, it is. Well, maybe I work in de fields with

Zee. And Pap gonna show me how to care for peaches and find the honey tree."

Pap's forgetting me already! Abby thought with a pang. Not that she blamed him. She was breaking his heart by leaving. Hopefully, Cyril would mend it.

"Then you need to know how to read a contract and write your name," Abby told him. "Or are you gonna just make an *X*?"

Cyril pondered the question. "No 'um, I needs to write my name. But you teach me, Abby. Not Missus."

"I'll teach you until I leave."

His eyes popped wide. "Where you goin'?"

"To Pennsylvania to live with my Mama."

"Why you want to go there? You gots everything you need right *here*."

"I doan have my Mama here," Abby explained. "An' Cyril, I love Hammond Plantation, but I also want to see more of the world."

Frowning, he scratched his head. "I doan understand."

Abby didn't know quite how to explain it because she wasn't sure herself. "You know how you love fishin' in the stream? Well, how 'bout if you had a great, wide river to fish in. Wouldn't that be excitin'?"

"Only if Pap and Lanny came with me."

Abby sighed. "I know what you mean." Traveling to

Tomasford with Mamie, Pap, and Mistress had been frightening enough. The thought of leaving her family and traveling alone to Pennsylvania gave her chilblains. *Oh how I'll miss them!*

Which was another reason she was having so much trouble writing that letter to her Mama. How could she just up and leave her home? Her family?

Then there was the sad news about Mamie. Her Mama was expecting them both. How could she tell Lively that her own mama was dead?

"'Sides, who's to say there better fish in de big river?" Cyril asked.

Abby cuffed him on the head. She was tired of his questions. They were too similar to the ones pushing and pulling in her own mind. It was like the war being fought all over again.

Cyril rubbed his head. "Ow. What that for?"

"To shut up your chatterin'," Abby said grumpily. "Now leave me alone so I can write my Mama an' tell her I'm comin'."

"Well, I ain sorry you leavin'," Cyril blurted and ran from the room before Abby could see his tears.

Abby set down the pen. *Oh, this tougher than splittin' kindling.* She knew leaving Hammond House would be sadder than anything. She knew traveling alone would be fearful. She knew writing about Mamie's death would be a sorrowful task. And she knew starting all over with her Mama would be joyfully hard. But something else was keeping her from writing. Something unspoken and ugly that hung in the air like skunk.

Gathering the letters, she headed from the Big House. She knew who would help her puzzle it out—the person who'd been there for her all her life: *Mamie.*

On the way to the cemetery, Abby peeked into the kitchen, hearing voices. Tissie was in front of the fireplace talking to a girl Abby didn't recognize.

"Abby, this Liza!" Tissie called to her. "Come say hi."

Curious, Abby came over. The girl was about fifteen with dusky skin and crinkled brown hair. "Hello, Liza."

"Liza from over de mountain," Tissie explained. "She's Zee's niece. She come to be in de weddin', den she'll stay and work at Hammond House. When you gone, I'm goin' to need help runnin' dis place."

"But I ain gone yet," Abby said, only Tissie was leading Liza out the kitchen door, saying, "Mister and Mistress eat in de Big House . . ."

Abby blinked hard. *It's like I'm already boardin' the train to Pennsylvania!*

Blowing out her breath, she fled the kitchen. Pap was in the garden hoeing beans. Abby waved at him with her free hand, hoping he wouldn't follow. She wanted to be alone with her grandma.

In the daylight, the cemetery was peaceful. Birds flitted from tree to tree and wildflowers poked up everywhere. Abby sank onto one of the sacks left beside the grave.

"Sorry I keep botherin' you, Mamie," she apologized. "But you the only one who I can talk to." Sitting cross-legged, Abby set the letters in her lap.

"I'm having a powerful hard time writin' my Mama," Abby explained. "Oh, Mamie, I want to go to her, but I doan want to leave you and Pap and my home. 'Cause you right, this *is* my home."

Sighing, she picked up two letters. "Then there's something else that has me truly befuddled, and I want to figure it out 'fore I write her." Clearing her throat, she read from the first letter, "*Tell Mistress Hammond that the past should hold us in bondage no longer. We must put the memories behind us and begin anew.*"

Abby refolded the letter. "Mistress said that Lively was furious with her when Mister forbid her to leave, so those words make sense. But see, Mamie, then there's *these* puzzling words." Abby read from the second letter, "*I promise that your secret is safe with me.*"

Pausing, she lay back on the sack, the letters on her chest, and stared at the clouds overhead. Was Mamie in Heaven, listening?

"What secret is Lively talkin' 'bout?" Abby asked

her. "An' I know you know the answer, Mamie, 'cause you told me on your deathbed that one reason you never shared the past was because you swore on the Bible you'd keep Mistress's secret. So Mamie, that's what's stickin' in my craw like a stone: *What is Mistress's secret?*"

Did her Mama's letters hold a clue? What had she missed in her exuberation over reading them?

Sitting up, Abby randomly plucked a letter from the pile and skimmed it. It was her Mama's latest letter, and as she read it, her eyes widened at the words: "We must put the memories of Kennedy's shooting behind us . . ."

Kennedy's shooting!

Lively's saying Kennedy had been shot? Only according to Mamie, Gabe killed Kennedy with his hands!

Abby closed her eyes, thinking back to Mamie's tale. "Forgive me, Lord," Mamie had murmured before telling how Gabe had killed Kennedy with his hands. *That* had been the lie. Gabe *hadn't* killed Kennedy! No slave, not even one as trusted as Gabe, would be allowed to carry a gun. That meant someone else shot and killed Kennedy.

Mister Hammond? Abby shook her head in doubt. Even coming upon Kennedy whipping Lively, Mister would have kept a cool head. He would have sent Kennedy packing or let the law deal with the man.

Then who?

"That's the secret, Mamie, ain it?" Abby asked the clouds. "The one you carried with you all these years. The one locked in Mistress's heart. Mamie, you have to tell me—who killed Kennedy?"

A dark shadow fell over Abby and she sprang up, the letters falling at her feet. "Mistress!"

"I was wondering when you would ask that question," Mistress said almost absently. She carried a basket as if gathering greens. "I knew it was inevitable—you're a clever girl, Abby. So I knew it was a matter of time before you'd discover the whole truth."

Abby stepped back. Was Mistress about to reveal the secret? Was it something horrible? Something Abby didn't really want to know?

Then she saw the tears in Mistress's eyes, and she knew that whatever the secret was it had been causing her pain all these years.

"I did puzzle some of it out," Abby said as she bent to gather the letters. "Gabe *didn't* kill Kennedy. An' I believe Mister didn't kill him either." Slowly, she straightened as a new thought struck her. "But Mistress, I believe you must have been there that night too."

With a moan, Mistress sank upon the sack at Abby's feet.

Abby clutched the letters to her chest, as the truth

hit her. "*You* shot Kennedy!" she gasped. "That's what Mamie meant by your secret."

Mistress nodded. Head bent, she sobbed silently.

Abby's mouth fell open. But at the same time, she wasn't surprised.

Without raising her head, Mistress said, "Kennedy was a brute. We all knew it. John was going to dismiss him as soon as harvest was over. That night, when I saw him beating your mother, I went as crazy as you father. Only *I* had a gun," she added, her voice suddenly steely.

"You saved my Mama's life," Abby whispered.

"Yes, but I killed a man." Mistress raised her head high. "I should have faced the courts with the truth. But John was afraid for me. I was a northerner. At that time, sentiment was already building against the North. And I'd killed a *white man* to protect a *slave*! It was unheard of!" Drawing up her knees like a child, she clasped her hands around her skirt. "John was afraid I'd go to jail. Gabe and Lively were the only true witnesses to what I'd done, and John assured their silence by offering them their freedom. We made up the story about Gabe running away, and Mister Hammond running Kennedy off the farm because he'd whipped Lively. Later, Mamie was brought in on the lies."

"But she found out the truth?" Abby guessed.

"Yes. I was babbling incoherently and John was distraught, worried about what might happen to me. The rest happened as I told it. John gave Gabe a letter of freedom and money to run away. His being caught and shot by slavecatchers later was a horrible accident. When Lively ran after him, Mamie was the only one left who knew the truth, and John assured her silence by threatening to sell you if she breathed a word."

Twisting sideways, Mistress pressed her palms against the grave. "Oh, Mamie. I'm so sorry. *I* caused Gabe to be killed. *I* drove away Lively. Then I hid her letters from you. *Everything* has been my fault!"

Stooping, Abby gently placed her hand on Mistress's arm. "Mistress, you doan need to apologize. Mamie know the real truth. She knowed why you killed Kennedy. Because you loved my Mama. That's why Mamie kept your secret. Not because she was afraid you'd sell me—she knew in her heart that you and Mister were too fair to do that—but because you saved Lively's life—and *mine.* An' *that's* why Lively forgive you, too. You would have known that if you read her last letter." She sorted through the pile until she found the latest letter. Unfolding it, she read, "'*Lastly, tell Mistress Rebecca I forgive her.*'"

"Your mother's still an exceptional woman," Mistress said. "And you're right, I need to accept her forgiveness—and forgive myself, although I'm not sure that's a possibility. However, there is something more important that I need to do. Something more urgent."

With a flurry of skirts, Mistress stood up. "Come, Abby, you have a letter to write. And then we have affairs to get in order, tickets to purchase, and bags to pack. Pennsylvania's a long journey."

Taken aback, Abby could only stare at her. "You're—you're going with me?" she stammered.

Mistress smiled. "Mamie would never forgive me if I sent her beloved 'chile' alone on a train to the north. Even one as smart and determined as you, Abby. Besides, I owe Lively an apology for thirteen years of lies and secrets. And a letter won't do. Oh, no, it won't do!"

"But Mistress, what about Mister Hammond? What about the crops? What about your home?"

"Now that Mister is feeling better, it's time he took charge. The burden has been on my shoulders long enough, don't you think? With Pap to guide him, and Zee and Tissie to manage the workers, I believe he'll do just fine."

Turning abruptly, Abby squatted beside the cross. "Only I'm not sure I can leave Mamie."

"Oh, Abby." Mistress crouched beside her. "I have no doubt your grandma will *never* leave you! She'll probably be guiding that train to Pennsylvania."

Abby grinned, realizing that Mistress was right. But

then another thought hit her just as hard. "Mistress, my Mama doan know me at all. What if I get there and she decides she doan love me?"

Placing one finger under Abby's chin, Mistress tipped up her head. Her expression was soulful. "Abby, she will love you. Not only because you're a fine person, but because she's your mother. I would give *anything* to hold Julia one more time, and I know Lively feels the same."

Abby nodded, too choked up to reply.

"Come." Standing, Mistress picked up her basket and turned toward the Big House. "Let's head back. There's much to plan."

Abby rose. She took one last look at Mamie's grave before falling into step beside Mistress. As they strolled back to the Big House, two odd companions discussing their trip, Abby felt a fire growing in her heart. This time it wasn't the fire of unanswered questions. It was the fire of freedom and of realized dreams.

Now she knew what to write in her letter.

Dear Mama,

I'm coming home!